HER
WEDDING NIGHT

It was a dark, rain-swept night when Donald Garth, silent and aloof, brought Penny, his bride of a few hours, to his ancestral home. In the great upper hall he flung open a door and stood courteously aside as she entered a small, jewel-like sitting room. Beyond it Penny—her heart heavy with the guilty lie she had told this man—saw the bedroom with pale yellow walls, enchantingly lovely in the soft light.

But Penny was hardly aware of all this luxury that was now hers. Panic-stricken, she wanted to run past this tall stranger who was her husband and escape into the night. If she remained, what would he demand of her? Would he expect her to go through with the tragic farce of marriage?

D1558760

Bantam Books by Emilie Loring
Ask your bookseller for the books you have missed

EMILIE LORING
I TAKE
THIS MAN

A NATIONAL GENERAL COMPANY

I TAKE THIS MAN

*A Bantam Book / published by arrangement with
Little, Brown and Company, Inc.*

PRINTING HISTORY

Little, Brown edition published January 1955
2nd printing .... March 1955
3rd printing .... March 1956

Grosset & Dunlap edition published February 1956
2nd printing ..... October 1956
3rd printing .... May 1957

Bantam edition published December 1958

2nd printing .... February 1961	*9th printing ... September 1965*
3rd printing .... January 1963	*10th printing .... October 1966*
4th printing .... June 1964	*11th printing .... April 1967*
5th printing .... June 1964	*12th printing ...... March 1968*
6th printing ..... August 1964	*13th printing .... June 1968*
7th printing ... November 1964	*14th printing .... October 1968*
8th printing .... April 1965	*15th printing ... August 1969*

16th printing ... December 1969

*Bantam Books are published by Bantam Books, Inc., a National
General company. Its trade-mark, consisting of the words "Bantam
Books" and the portrayal of a bantam, is registered in the United
States Patent Office and in other countries. Marca Registrada.
Bantam Books, Inc., 666 Fifth Avenue, New York, N.Y. 10019.*

PRINTED IN THE UNITED STATES OF AMERICA

I TAKE THIS MAN

I

How the minutes raced! If she could only hold them back. The white-faced girl confronted herself in the mirror. The shining surface reflected soft, almost black hair under a small, smart hat; dark eyes that were normally brilliant but were dulled with heartache; a soft red mouth shaped for smiling but somber now. It reflected the dark-blue velvet dress, the jaunty feather set in the hat, the sable stole.

She lifted her hand to her throat as though she were choking and the mirror reflected back the circlet of diamonds that flashed on the third finger of the looking-glass girl's left hand. With a sharp exclamation she made a movement as though to tear it off and then turned away from the mirror and walked blindly to the window.

She was married, irrevocably married. She who had been Penelope Sherrod was now Penelope Garth. It had happened, really happened. All along she had deceived herself, she had believed that it couldn't happen, that some miraculous turn of the wheel of fortune would save her at the last moment. And then her dream world had been rudely shattered when, half an hour before, she heard the voice of the clergyman say solemnly, "Do you take this man to be your wedded husband?"

"I do," she had answered. She had spoken the words that separated her forever from Dick Wentworth.

It was done now. There was no going back to yesterday. No going back to Penelope Sherrod. No going back to the dream that Dick would find a way to save her from marriage to Donald Garth. Every telephone call, every ring at the doorbell, every letter, every meeting with Dick had renewed the hope that he would say eagerly, "Penny, you won't have to marry him. Because I can look after your mother. I can pay for her operation. Something wonderful has happened. I've just been left a fortune. An uncle has left me a lot of money. I've got a terrific job. It's all right, Penny."

But nothing wonderful happened and it hadn't been all right. Even when she had poured out the story of her mother's desperate illness, of the long and expensive care she must have without delay if her life were to be saved, Dick had had no suggestion to offer. If he hadn't been Dick, if she hadn't loved him so much that she could see no fault in him, she would have been humiliated by the tears she had shed on his shoulder, by the fact that she had let him guess how much she wanted him to find the solution for her, how deeply she loved him.

Now she must put Dick out of her life, try to forget him— as though she ever could. Mrs. Donald Garth. Remember, she told herself fiercely, you are Mrs. Donald Garth. The past is gone. You've got to build the future yourself.

She turned back to the girl in the mirror. You don't look much like a bride, she scolded herself. You must do better than that. She forced a wavering, uncertain smile to her lips. It would not do to go down the stairs and meet the wedding guests and her mother's loving eyes with that shadowed, tragic face. If her mother were to guess that she was marrying without love, were to worry about her, she would have less chance of coming successfully through her operation than if she went into it with her mind free, confident about her beloved daughter's future happiness.

Penelope held her head high and this time the smile was brighter, more convincing. And then she remembered that among the wedding guests was Dick Wentworth, who had sat white-faced and thoughtful during the ceremony. She would have to see him as she ran out of the house with Donald, a happy bride and groom setting out on their wedding journey.

I can't, she moaned to herself. I can't run past him, laughing. Why, oh, why did Dick insist on coming to the wedding? It would have been so much easier if he had stayed away.

To give herself time before meeting her ordeal, she looked slowly around the room. This was the house in which she had been born and had grown up, the house that was to be closed permanently tomorrow when her mother went to the hospital. And with it would close the door to Penny's happy, carefree girlhood.

Within these familiar walls she and her younger brother Terence had laughed and squabbled and pored over their books and confided their bright dreams for the future. Thank heaven, she told herself fervently, Terry did not suspect her feeling for Dick Wentworth. He had an attitude amounting almost to hero worship for—for her husband, she forced herself to say. Her husband. Donald Garth.

One—two—three—down you go, she forced herself to laugh back at the girl in the mirror with an attempt at gaiety.

2

She squared her shoulders, lifted her chin. She gave a start, her heart thudded as the door was flung open violently and Nora came in. Because of Mrs. Sherrod's frail health, Penny's old nurse had graduated to the position of being general factotum, cook, housekeeper and deputy mother to the Sherrod youngsters. She was a large woman with a round, unlined face, cheeks as pink as a girl's and soft brown hair only lightly dusted with gray. Penny and Terry had adored her all their lives. In their loving eyes, Nora had only two shortcomings: she moved around the house like a hurricane, doors and windows flying open and banging shut as though a cyclone struck them at her approach; and she continued to treat them as though they were small children.

A minor problem in relation to Penny's marriage had been the fate of Nora. With the house closed, what would become of her? Donald Garth had promptly settled this to everyone's satisfaction by suggesting that Nora come to Uplands, his family home where Penny was to live, as her young mistress's personal maid. As a result, Nora was now as much Donald's devoted slave as Terry.

In fact, Penny thought rebelliously, everyone believed Donald Garth was perfect. Everyone but—his wife. To her he was only an extremely handsome older man who had proved to be a pleasant companion during the days of his courtship. A little aloof. She realized now that he had rarely kissed her and only in a brotherly way. Basically, he had remained a stranger.

To Penny's surprise, her old nurse was flushed with anger, her cheeks as bright as a peony, her eyes sending out sparks. As she looked at Penny her wrath died down; she smiled tremulously, her eyes wet with tears.

"My little Penny a bride." Her voice was tender. Her big calloused hand touched the girl's cheek lovingly, in a lingering caress. "I always knew you'd be a beautiful bride. Those long lashes make your eyes look all shadowy somehow. There's a graver look about you. Perhaps," she added wisely, "it's because you've grown up today."

Penny turned away from the shrewd eyes that knew her so well and picked up her gloves and handbag. "Well," she said shakily, "I guess it's time to go." She reached for her fragrant wedding bouquet. "I mustn't forget to throw this to my bridesmaids. I wonder which one will catch it? I suspect Nancy will be the next to marry." She forced a gay laugh.

"There now," Nora said in relief, "I knew all the time that it was just nonsense."

3

"What is nonsense?"

"What that Wentworth man was saying to me," Nora replied with a snort of disgust.

Penny's heart turned over. "Dick—Wentworth?" she half whispered.

Nora nodded vigorously. "Got hold of me downstairs," she declared. "He gave me a song and dance. Said he had to see you. I asked him, 'See Penny now, when she's dressing to go on her honeymoon?' And he told me he had to see you. Kept repeating it. *Had* to see you." Once more anger flushed the nurse's face.

"W-well," Penny stuttered. "T-then w-what?"

"He even dared to tell me that you would say so, too. He said he loved you and he had to see you once more. And when I said what right had he to say he loved you, now you're married—if he ever had such a right, which I doubted very much—he said—" Nora fairly choked in her fury—"he said you loved him too. He had to see you this once."

With one of her vigorous movements she banged against a small table, nearly knocking it over. Even in her breathless interest in what the older woman had to say, Penny smiled faintly at her familiar, noisy clumsiness.

Nora had really worked herself up by this time. "To say you loved him! A likely thing. And why would you be marrying Mr. Garth, I asked him, if you loved the likes of him. And the Wentworth man said it was because he didn't have any money. I wonder now I didn't show him the back of my fist. If you want me to, I'll have him put out of the house without wasting another minute. Sure, Terry would make quick work of him. And Mr. Garth—it would do my heart good to see what was left of the Wentworth man when Mr. Garth got through with him."

She started toward the door. "I'll just have a word with young Terry."

"Nora! No!" Penny cried in protest. "You can't do that. It would be cruel. He's unhappy enough. And stop calling him the Wentworth man, as though—"

The kindly eyes that studied the girl's face widened. Before that searching scrutiny Penny's eyes wavered, fell. She turned her head away. She did not speak.

Nora took a long breath. "It's true then," she said flatly.

Penny's eyes were brilliant with tears that hung on the long lashes, rolled down her cheeks. To her surprise, Nora, from whom she had never known anything but affectionate kindness, stiffened, seemed to withdraw from her.

4

"I saw you born, Penny, and I've brought you up almost as much as your own mother. And felt almost the same, too. I'd have staked my life neither you nor Terry could do a dishonorable thing. Mistaken, maybe, but not dishonorable."

"Dishonorable!" Penny flinched as though Nora had struck her.

"Dishonorable," the old woman repeated firmly. "To marry one man when you loved another. Why?" She took the girl's chin with her hand, turning her head, forcing her to face her. "Why?"

"Because——" Penny threw out her hands in a helpless gesture. "Because Dick hasn't any money and——"

"I can't believe it of you. To marry for money, to marry without love."

"If you'd only let me explain," Penny wailed. "It's not for me. I don't want the money for myself. I'd rather starve. You ought to know that. It's for Mother. You know she has to have that operation and months and months of expensive treatments. And there was no money, no possible way—and Dick—he'd have helped me if he could—only—he didn't have the money or a job——"

"And he hasn't been looking for a job that I've noticed," Nora snapped. After a moment she sighed. "So that's it." She was silent again for a long time. "I don't know," she admitted at last, "what you should have done. But I know what you should do now. Tell your husband the truth." She brushed her hand across her wet eyes. "And I thought you were a happy bride."

"Don't worry about me. I don't matter in this," Penny assured her gallantly. "It will be all right, really it will."

"That's my girl. Whatever comes I know you will face it with gay courage. I trust——"

She broke off. A man stood in the doorway, white-faced and tense.

"I thought," he said, his voice cautiously low, "you were going to send Penny to me."

At the sound of his voice Penny whirled around. "Dick!" It was a half-stifled cry. "Dick, I'm married now. I can't see you any more."

He glanced at Nora and said, "This is the last time, Penny. Let me say good-by."

Nora looked from Penny to the man she loved. "I'll tell them you'll be down in five minutes," she said and went out. For once she did not bang the door behind her.

Penny looked incredulously at the man before her. His blue

5

eyes burned like coals. He was slight and fair-haired, with an easy charm that had always smoothed his way through life. His mother had spoiled him, his aunts had indulged him, his teachers had been indulgent with him, girls had been mad about him. At the moment he was nervous, the finger that touched his small mustache trembled.

He came forward and took her hands in his. "Penny," he cried. "Penny, my darling."

Penny took a step backward and withdrew her hands, holding him off. "Dick," she warned him, "I am married now."

"But you love me." There was a hint of triumph in his voice.

"You can't stay here," she said brokenly, "and I can't see you again, Dick. Good-by," her voice wavered, "and good luck."

"You'll see me," he promised. "Remember—we love each other. When two people love each other, life cannot separate them. Somehow or other—"

"Stop! You must not say another word. You aren't talking to Penelope Sherrod now. You are speaking to Donald Garth's wife."

"Donald Garth's wife," he repeated bitterly. "Bought and paid for. Garth has always had everything without needing to lift a hand for it. He inherited Uplands, one of the show places of the nation; he inherited the Works, the biggest manufacturing plant for airplanes in America, bringing in a fortune every year; he got you." Wentworth's tone changed. He added quietly, "But he didn't get your love, Penny. That, at least, belongs to me."

"But we must forget that," she reminded him. "I intend to do my best to be—a good wife. I can at least give Don loyalty."

"Penny," he said in a tone she had never heard from him before, "I want you to listen to me. Things are not over between us. We will meet again and again. After all, we belong to the same social set. To avoid meeting would simply make people suspicious. When you return from your wedding trip and get established at Uplands, I'll be visiting there." He smiled with an arrogant confidence. "And after a few months of Garth you'll be glad to see me, Penny. I can promise you that. The future belongs to me—to us."

Penny looked at him, feeling that she had never seen him before. This was a bad dream, a nightmare. In a moment she would awaken and find that the unforgivable words had not been spoken. Dick could not be saying these ugly things.

6

Could not be thinking them. Had he always been like this? How could she have been so blind?

"Go, Dick," she said crisply. "You'll never be invited to Uplands. Never! To believe, for a single moment, that after marrying Don I would not be loyal to him, in thought as well as in deed, is an insult I wouldn't have believed you capable—"

"Penny!" He took a step forward. He said soothingly, "You're all upset and excited. You don't know what you are saying."

"I know exactly what I am saying."

Nora's heavy tread was heard on the stairs. Dick paused indecisively and then, at Penny's gesture, went out of the room. At the door he turned, summoned up a smile. "I'll be seeing you."

II

Penny sagged limply against a chair. That was Dick Wentworth! That was the man she had loved. And he dared to assume, to speak to her as though, married to another man, she would still be willing to see him; probably even, in a matter of months, possibly weeks, turn to him for one of those furtive, dishonest love affairs which she had always loathed.

She felt shamed and humiliated, shamed that Dick could so misjudge her, humiliated to think she had given her love to a man so unworthy of it. For his sake she had cheated Donald Garth of the love she owed him as his wife.

Nora came in. She looked anxiously at Penny's haggard face. "Are you ready to go down?" she asked gently.

Penny nodded. She was speechless. Try as she would she could not force a single word from her tight throat.

"Mr. Garth's been dressing in Terry's room next door. I'll just see if he's ready. But first—" the older woman hesitated—"don't disappoint me, Penny. Don't go on with this marriage while there is a lie between you. Tell your husband the truth, that you don't love him, that you married him to—"

"Don't worry, Nora, he does know it," interrupted a grave voice.

Instinctively, Nora drew closer to the girl whom she had protected all her young life. She felt Penelope's slender fingers grip hers, saw her face and lips turn parchment white as she

7

turned to look up at the tall man who stood in the doorway between the two rooms.

My husband, Penny thought in a sick panic. My husband. Donald Garth was fine-looking, a *grand seigneur* to his finger tips. His face was as colorless as Penny's but he held himself erect, poised, completely under control, grave and unexpectedly formal. It seemed to Penny that during the brief interval in which their eyes met an invisible wall grew up between them, faster and taller than Jack's beanstalk, so wide and high and thick that nothing would ever break it down again.

"Sorry," he told his young bride with stern courtesy, as though addressing a stranger whom he had just met rather than his wife of an hour, "I was dressing in Terry's room. The door was slightly ajar and I couldn't avoid overhearing some of your conversation with—" he swallowed and for a brief moment he seemed to have difficulty in keeping his voice steady, coldly impersonal—"with Nora and Wentworth."

A smile lighted his eyes for a moment as he looked at the maid.

"Has my car come around, Nora?"

She looked at him with frightened eyes, ready to defend Penny if necessary, not certain of his mood. "It's waiting, sir."

He was gay as he gave his orders to the startled woman. "The bride and groom are coming down. Tell the guests to be ready with the confetti. Remember, this is a joyous occasion, a great festivity. A time for celebration and happiness."

Hearing the somber mockery in his voice, Penny felt that he was cutting her with little knives.

With a sharp glance at the girl, Nora went down the stairs and the two motionless people could hear her calling, "They're coming! They're coming!"

The smile faded from Donald Garth's eyes and his face was bleak when he turned back to Penny. She still leaned against the chair for support. She looked up at the man she had married, his gray eyes looking almost black, his firm lips set in an expression she had never before seen on his face. His hands were clenched in an effort at control, until they showed white at the knuckles.

"I'd like—to tell you about it," she ventured, a break in her voice.

"I've heard most of it," he said in a voice he had never used to her before. "I lived hours in that room. I've known—from the time we became engaged—I've known that you didn't love me as you are capable of loving. That's why I

8

didn't—hurry you, didn't try to make love to you. I wanted to give you time. Like a fool, I thought in time I could teach you to love me. I had no suspicion that there was anyone else. And Wentworth—" his voice was icy with contempt —"that's the kind of man you love."

Color spread in a hot wave to her forehead and she turned away. She wanted to say that she did not blame him for his contempt, that she deserved it, that she was ashamed of the love she had given Dick Wentworth, that it had died between one moment and the next. But how could she expect him to believe it? She herself had not known that love could die so completely, in a flash. One glimpse into the depths of Dick Wentworth's soul, one clear vision of the hollow man within, and it was over.

But Donald Garth would never believe her! He had heard her admit her love a few minutes earlier. He would laugh at her. His contempt would deepen, if that were possible.

She stood quietly before Donald Garth, slender, lovely, tragic. She was acutely conscious of his hands that held her arms so ruthlessly. After all, there was nothing that she could say. Whether or not her love for Dick Wentworth was dead, she had still injured her husband in a way she could not repair, she had married him without love.

"Don," she said quickly, before she could lose her precarious courage, "I meant it when I said I would try to be a good wife."

His fine-cut lips curled. There was scorn in his voice when he answered hotly, "Did you think for a moment I would want a woman whose heart is filled by another man?"

Her dark eyes met his steadily. "Does that mean that you will divorce me?"

He looked into their depths and shook his head. His voice was rough and compelling as he answered, "Divorce? No. You and I have made a solemn compact, Penelope. We'll keep it. At least, before the world." There was a touch of bitterness in his voice now. He controlled it by an effort of will.

"An hour ago I took a vow. I took this woman to be my wedded wife, to have and to hold from this day forward, for better for worse, for richer for poorer, in sickness and in health, to love and to cherish, till death us do part."

The beauty of the words as he spoke them left her too shaken for a reply. He went on, "Marriage means something to me. What it meant to my parents and their parents and all the generations before them. Most of them were happy marriages, rich and warm and adventurous with love. But the few that were not happy were, at least, a success before the world. They had dignity and self-respect and loyalty."

For the first time Penelope was acutely conscious of the personality of the man she had married. He had strength, will power, determination, great force. He was not a man to be tricked. Not a man, she realized painfully, to be satisfied with second best.

"You will come away with me as we planned," he said clearly. "We will—cancel our honeymoon plans—that would be too much of a farce—and return immediately to Uplands. You will conduct yourself there as my—as the woman I have married should. If I have not acquired a wife, at least Uplands has a mistress and I have a hostess."

Tears brimmed over in her eyes, rolled down her cheeks. "It's all so unfair to you."

He raised his eyebrows. "A little late to think of that, isn't it? At least, I still have the Works to keep me busy. They will give me a purpose in life."

He released her abruptly as though conscious for the first time of the steel grip with which he had held her.

"About your mother," he said more gently, "everything will be done that can possibly be done. You know that without my telling you. I've settled an income on you so you will be independent—"

"No, Don!" she cried, pride and anger in her voice. "For my mother—yes. But not for myself. Not one cent."

His eyes held hers. "You have married me. In the eyes of the world you are my wife. As my wife, if I can expect nothing else from you, I will expect you to uphold your position. I insist upon it. As mistress of Uplands, as hostess for the people I expect to entertain, people who have been my friends and neighbors for years, frequently diplomats from foreign countries and the leaders of our own, you will find it necessary to spend a certain amount of money. You must not humiliate me further."

Her pride was outraged. She would not accept his money. She could not. And then she thought: But Don has pride too. Certainly, it is only fair to swallow mine, to leave him his pride when I have taken away everything else.

"All right, Don," she choked.

He nodded grimly. "Now let's go down and have the wedding guests speed the happy bride and groom on their way."

"Don't lash me any more with your tongue," she whispered.

10

"I know I deserve it. I know I deserve more than that. But my heart feels as though it has been flayed to ribbons."

It was true, but the flaying had been done not by the loss of her faith in Dick Wentworth but by Garth's tongue. The intolerable ache that had been in her heart when she had entered this room after the ceremony to take off her wedding dress was gone. Gone like her blind infatuation for Wentworth. Bruised and sore as it was, her heart was curiously light. Penny could not understand it herself.

Garth took her hand and they ran down the stairs side by side, laughing, joking, kissing and being kissed as the guests surrounded them. Anyone, the girl thought, would take them for the happiest couple in the world. She was seized in her brother's arms and kissed jubilantly.

"Good-by, Terry," she said, summoning up a brilliant smile.

" 'By, Lucky Penny. Don, take good care of her. But I don't need to say that to you. I'd rather see her in your hands than with anyone else in the world."

"Thanks, Terry." Garth grinned at his young brother-in-law but his lips were ashen.

For a tender moment Penny was in her mother's arms. " 'By for a little while, Marmee," she whispered. "Thanks for everything you've done and been. You're going to be well and fat and sassy next time I see you."

Her frail mother smiled reassuringly. "Of course I shall," she promised, as though there were not the shadow of a doubt as to her recovery. "And you, Penny. I won't say I want your happiness. You know that. I will just say—God grant that you will be a good and true wife."

Garth drew his wife, laughing, down the steps, ducking a shower of rice and confetti. The touch of his fingers around her hand made it tingle. Then he released her, they were in the car and it was moving smoothly along the drive. She stole a glance at his face. The laughter was gone. It was set, withdrawn. She was married to a stranger, and yet she had known him most of her life.

Always he had been more remote than an older brother because great wealth and vast industrial responsibility had matured him more quickly than the other young men she had known. Not until she had returned from school had he seemed to pay any attention to her. Theirs had not been a storm-shaking courtship; rather a friendship which had ripened slowly until the day when he had asked her to be his wife.

Her face burned when she remembered telling Dick Went-

11

worth her problem, telling him of her mother's grave illness and her pressing need for money. He had been sorry but he had not had any suggestion to offer. So she had accepted Garth. And now Dick was waiting confidently for the day when she would turn from her husband to him.

Somehow she had to make up to Donald Garth for the great wrong she had done him. She looked at the stern, clean-cut profile. He seemed older now than his thirty-one years, only eight years older than she was.

"Don," she said unsteadily, "can we ever be good friends again?"

He kept his eyes on the road. "Friends," he said briefly, "are people you trust."

He increased the speed of the car.

III

The honeymoon trip was to have taken them to Arizona and New Mexico to escape from cold and dampness into warmth and dazzling sunshine. Instead, Garth canceled the reservations, telephoned instructions to his domestic staff at Uplands, and the silent couple drove there through the rain.

There was no sound in the car but the steady swish of the windshield wipers. Garth had withdrawn as far from his bride as though he were on another planet. He sat with his hands steady on the wheel, his eyes on the road. Beside him Penny, too, was silent. There seemed to be no way at all to reach him. If only they could be friends! It was, she decided, she who had destroyed the foundations of their friendship. She would have to be the one to build it up again. At the moment she could see no possible way of doing it.

Friends are people you trust. Don's words were like a sword in her heart. *Dishonorable.* That had been Nora's judgment. The words tortured her. What could I have done, she cried out to herself. I couldn't have let Marmee die for lack of care. And what else was there to do?

God grant that you will be a good and true wife. Her mother's prayer for her hurt more than anything else could possibly do. The wrong was done now, the wrong to Donald Garth. Somehow, some way, she must make it up to him. In some fashion she must pay the vast debt she owed him, pay

12

for her mother's health, pay for having defrauded him of the love he had hoped for when he married her.

I'll find a way, she told herself steadily. I'll find a way. Some day even Nora will admit I am honorable; some day even Marmee will know I am a good and true wife; some day even Don will believe that I am to be trusted.

As Garth slowed for a deep pool of water on the road and eased the car through it, she realized, with a start of surprise, that for the first time in months she had forgotten Dick Wentworth. His spell was broken forever and she was free of him.

It was dark when Garth swept between the gateposts at Uplands and turned up the curving driveway to the house. The door opened with a blaze of golden light like a path in the night and the butler hastened down the steps carrying a big umbrella. Penny went up the steps under its shelter, hardly aware of the house in her haste to escape the rain, and in a few moments Garth joined her.

The servants had assembled in the main hall to welcome her: Fane, the butler; Mrs. Brown, the housekeeper; Garth's valet, Macy; the cook, housemaids and chauffeur. If they were surprised by the sudden shift in the honeymoon plans, there was no indication of it. In a lightning preparation for the couple, the great hall with its magnificent branching staircase was massed with flowers.

Again Garth made a quick and convincing change. Just as he had altered from the laughing bridegroom saying good-by to the wedding guests into the silent man who had driven her to Uplands, so now the sternness melted from his face. He took her hand, smiling at his staff.

"This is my wife," he said. "I know that you will all do everything in your power to meet her wishes."

He introduced them one at a time and Penny shook hands, smiling, saying a pleasant word to each of them. As she did so, she became aware that the position of Garth's wife entailed more responsibilities than she had known. The servants were smiling and friendly and obviously delighted with their employer's pretty wife. But there were exceptions. While she liked and trusted at once the level-eyed chauffeur, the smiling housemaids, the motherly cook, she realized that the housekeeper was accustomed to running the establishment to suit herself and that she would not brook any interference without a struggle. Fane, the butler, his face as flat as a saucer, thin-lipped and gimlet-eyed, watched her with a keen scrutiny that took her by surprise. And for Macy, Garth's valet, a ferret-faced man, she felt an instinctive distrust.

13

Garth, still smiling, led her up the staircase and along a corridor. At the end he flung open the door of a small sitting room, with copper-colored walls, flowers everywhere, and French windows which opened on a small balcony, rain-drenched now.

Beyond was a bedroom with pale yellow walls, and blue upholstery and coverings on bed, chaise lounge and chairs.

The rooms were enchantingly lovely but Penny was hardly aware of them. She was married to Donald Garth, she had come to his home to live as his wife. For one panicky moment she wanted to run past him, to escape out into the rain, to go anywhere, anyhow. What terrible thing had she done? And now she was trapped.

What would he expect of her? Would the tall, rigid man at her side take her in his arms? Would he expect her to go through with the tragic farce of marriage? She forced herself to look at him.

Garth's smile was gone. He glanced around the suite of rooms to see that his orders had been carried out, said, "I hope you will be comfortable here, Penelope."

She opened her lips. She must say something. She must, at least, say the rooms were lovely, the flowers beautiful and welcoming.

Before she could speak he said formally, "Good night." The door closed behind him.

ii

The door closed behind him. After a moment's indecision Don went down the corridor to his bedroom which adjoined Penny's. Without bothering to turn on the lights he walked to the window and stood, hands thrust into his pockets, staring blindly into the black night, the sound of the rain loud in his ears.

And this was his wedding night! He gave a short, mirth-less laugh and turned away from the window. Changed to slacks and sweater and a raincoat. Went noiselessly down the stairs and let himself out a side door quietly so that the servants would not be aware of the strange behavior of the bride-groom.

He walked up and down the garden path, thinking of Penny. He saw her walking up the church aisle toward him, her wedding veil floating like a mist. More beautiful than he had ever seen her. He'd thought of Tennyson's words:

14

Clothed in white samite, mystic, wonderful. And wondered what samite was. Her small hand had rested in his own. Icy cold. And she had spoken her vows in a steady voice.

And all the time she had thought, as she had said later: I'd rather starve!

Rain beat on his bare head as he tramped back and forth. *I'd rather starve. Rather starve.* And worst of all was Dick Wentworth's voice saying, "But he didn't get your love, Penny."

No, Don told himself savagely, I didn't get her love. Why didn't I let her go when I knew how she felt? No. No! I'll never let her go.

Rather starve, said her voice in his ear. *I'll be seeing you*, came the echo of Wentworth's last confident words.

Don plunged on, wishing the sound of the rain would drown out the mocking sound of the voices. And he saw Penny in her blue velvet dress, saw her eyes pleading for his forgiveness, saw her loveliness that wrenched his heart.

All during the courtship he had been gentle and patient because he had known she did not love him as he wanted to be loved. But time and tenderness, he had thought, would awaken her to love. And instead she had loved Wentworth! Wentworth. A fortune hunter, a fellow who refused to get a job, to carry responsibility. A drifter.

"He shan't have her," Donald Garth vowed to himself. "He shan't have her. And if he dares come to Uplands—"

He turned back toward the house he loved. The lighted windows above were Penny's. His wife. His head went back. I'll win her all over again, he decided. But this time I'll do it differently.

iii

Weeks later, Penny stood at the window in the drawing room at Uplands staring out into the rain. For the past half-hour she had been pacing up and down restlessly. There was nothing for her to do. The housekeeper controlled the smooth running of Uplands. So far the girl's duties had consisted of checking the daily menus, of sitting across the dinner table from Garth at night, making conversation as long as Fane and the waitress were in the room, lapsing into brooding silence when they were left alone.

That was the only time she saw her stranger husband. Breakfast was served to her on a tray in bed, and Don had left the house long before she got up. She had suggested

15

tentatively, shyly, joining him for breakfast but he had vetoed the suggestion so coldly that she did not make it again.

The Works seemed to absorb all his time and his attention. All day he spent at his desk at the plant his grandfather had built; his evenings were occupied at his desk in his study at Uplands. Such free time as he had he spent with Geoffrey Jarvis, a college friend and now a neighbor.

Penny's lips twisted bitterly as she realized that she had no importance, no function at Uplands. She was nothing but a guest in the house. She had no real place there at all. It would almost be better if Donald would quarrel with her. Perhaps that would clear the air. But he maintained a cold, formal courtesy that never altered, never warmed for a moment into friendship.

Problems, perplexities and heartaches are sufficiently pervasive when the sun shines, but give them a long stretch of dull, wet weather in which to thrive and they take possession of every nook and cranny of the mind, weaken the judgment, invade sleeping hours and grow and grow until their rank luxuriance smothers all sense of proportion.

Penelope Garth was quite conscious that she was seeing small things big and big things small as she stared down from the window onto the rain-drenched garden. In the weeks since her marriage there had been only one day of sunshine. Try as she would, she could not seem to get her grip. She felt as though she had been swept out to sea without rudder or compass or mental stamina enough to save herself from being dashed on the rocks of disaster.

The girl turned restlessly from the window and dropped into the big chair in front of the fire. The soft pink of the cushions and hangings radiated a rosy glow which made one forget the dripping world outside. The color and comfort struck a tiny spark of warmth in Penelope's heart which felt so hard and cold these days. The only bright spot was that her mother had weathered the critical operation, "almost miraculously," her nurse wrote, and, though still very weak, she was improving every day. As soon as she could be moved, she was going south, attended by the nurse, where she could have a long, leisurely convalescence.

Marmee is going to live, the girl told herself. Whatever happens to me, surely that was worth doing. And how else could I have managed it? How else? But remembering Don's frigid courtesy she thought with a pang: I've done it at his expense. I've hurt him so that she could live. At times it was desperately hard to know what was right, what was wrong.

16

She gazed unblinkingly at the red coals and let her thoughts trail back over the long days she had spent at Uplands. She could not go on in this listless, idle way. She must have an absorbing personal task. There was no likelihood that the responsibility for managing Uplands would be put in her hands. The domestic machinery of the great house in which she and Donald lived ran with the perfection of clockwork. So it had run in the lifetime of Garth's father and of his father before him. The housekeeper carried matters with a high hand and resented suggestions.

If she could not manage the house—what then? Not merely her pride was at stake, although, since Donald insisted that she accept the income he had settled on her, she longed to feel that she was earning it in some way. But more than that, she felt that every human being must find useful work of some kind to do, in order to justify existence. She had no creative talents for the arts but everything a person can do, Marmee had told her long before, can be made creative. Whether you cultivate a garden or become a truly fine and reliable friend or prepare an attractive and appetizing meal—it can be made a creative act.

She stretched out her small feet to the blaze and clasped her hands behind her head. Her brows puckered in perplexity. There is something you can do, Penny Sherrod—Penny Garth, she corrected herself. There is some way you can be useful in the world instead of just a—just a guest.

If not at Uplands—then the Works? At that enormous plant there must be a job she could fill. But Don would never permit it. There would be too much comment, gossip, if Mrs. Donald Garth were to become an employee at the Works.

She picked up the newspaper which she had cast aside when her rebellious thoughts drove her to the window. This time she put aside her own problems and considered the meaning of what she had read. On the whole, the state of the world made her own worries seem trivial. Again her mind returned to the thought that there must be something useful she could do. The world was seething with distrust, danger was imminent, not only for nations but for civilization itself. In times like these everyone had a job to do, trying to strengthen such bonds of understanding as there were, to build a safe world and sound, enlightened citizenship.

Soon, she knew, her brother Terry would be in the armed services. She was glad that he had been able to finish college first and, though he joked about it, she knew that he had made a brilliant record. Terry a soldier, Terry sent away to

17

a distant part of the disturbed world to fight. Her throat tightened.

She stared unseeingly at the fire. You don't have to go out into the world to do something useful, she told herself. For a person with eyes to see, there is always something close at hand. Misery, loneliness, sickness, fear.

She sat bolt upright, her eyes snapping. There was the village! The Works had expanded so much and so fast that the village and surrounding sections were overcrowded. There were any number of things needed and needed badly: nursery schools for babies whose mothers were working; playgrounds for older children to help combat the growing tragedy of juvenile delinquency; classes to teach mothers homemaking, menu-planning for a proper diet so that youngsters would grow with straight legs and sound nerves and plenty of energy, cooking—home decorating to make even the humblest place beautiful.

The project opened out so rapidly, so dazzlingly that Penny was dazed by it. At last she had found a field in which she could be useful. And, indirectly, at least, Don would reap the benefit because it would be the families of his employees who would be helped.

She heard Fane's voice in the hallway and found herself listening alertly even while she wondered at the distrust she felt for the impeccable butler. Then she heard a familiar voice that brought her to her feet with a joyous cry, "Terry!"

A moment later, Terence Sherrod poked his head in at the open door. The room was dusky, the firelight illumined the figure of his sister where she stood, hands out, waiting for him.

"Gosh, Penny. It's as dark as a pocket! What's the great idea?"

" 'Fraid of the dark?" she mocked him as she pressed a switch and flooded the place with light. It was a stalwart young figure she saw, tall, with some of the awkwardness of youth, hair tousled, eyes steady, mouth still boyish but already showing the control of maturity.

"And how is Mrs. Garth?" he asked her gaily but his eyes were serious, watchful, convincing himself that his adored sister was happy.

Watch your step, Penny, the girl warned herself. Terry must not suspect that all is not well between you and Don.

She laughed at him. "Wonderful," she said. "It's a wonderful world. And Marmee?"

"I've just been to see her," the boy said. "She was sitting up in bed. She looked so little and frail but she was as gay as

18

ever. You'd never think she'd faced any trouble or pain. And the nurse says she'll be strong and well if she has the right kind of care. It may take months but she'll win through."

Penny smiled at him through wet lashes. "She will win through," she promised him.

The boy gave her a quick hug. "It's good to see you." His face fell. "Gosh, Penny," he added ruefully, "I didn't stop to think I was walking in on a honeymoon. How dumb can you get?"

"You aren't," Penny said impulsively and could have bitten out her tongue. "I mean, you aren't coming where you aren't wanted."

"That's swell. Now that the house is closed up for good I guess I'll be thinking of Uplands as home. That is, when I can get here."

A self-conscious note in his voice made his sister look at him in alarm. "What does that mean?"

"Uncle Sam has just sent me a special invitation," he said lightly.

"Oh, Terry!" She strangled back the sob which seemed to tear from her heart, turned it into an exclamation of excitement. She flung her arms around him.

"There, there, that's all right." He patted her hair with hearty, loving lack of consideration for the possible effect on its arrangement. "Say, what time do we eat? I've been driving all day and I won't do a thing to a square meal."

"Dinner in an hour," she said. "Hurry along to your room and make yourself presentable. Macy will provide anything you need."

"Where's Don?"

"Probably at Geoffrey Jarvis's cottage. He'll be home in time for dinner."

She did not add that Don spent whatever free time he had with his close friend at the latter's cottage a mile from Uplands. Geoff must wonder, she thought sometimes, why Don chose to devote his leisure to his friend rather than to his bride. Or had Don told him the truth about their relationship? She answered the question immediately in her mind. Don would not say a word. The marriage was to be played out before the world.

That night, for the first time since she had come to Uplands, Penelope arrayed herself for dinner in one of her trousseau evening gowns. So far she had worn old dinner dresses with long sleeves because the marks which Don's fingers had made on the soft flesh above her elbows on the day of their marriage still showed faintly blue. But now she believed that no one would detect them.

The soft yellow dress with its flecks of gold was more becoming to her than she had remembered. Excitement and pleasure over Terry's arrival had brought color to her cheeks and a sparkle to her eyes.

There was a tap at her bedroom door which adjoined Don's room, and in answer to her "Come in," the door opened for the first time since her arrival. Don was meticulously dressed in a perfectly fitted dinner jacket that molded the broad shoulders and made the most of his superb carriage. He held a square silver box in his hands.

As Penny turned to face him he came forward and laid the box on her dressing table. Beside it he placed a small key.

"These were my mother's jewels," he said. "I intended them for you—" there was a momentary bitter twist to his lips—"from the moment I first saw you. They would have been in your hands sooner but the settings were old-fashioned and Cartier's have been cleaning and resetting them. I would appreciate it," he added formally, "if you could find something that pleased you to wear tonight."

He turned swiftly and had returned to his own room, the door closing with a decisive click, before she could speak.

For a moment Penny stood looking at the door. The key was on her side, and though she had never locked the door Garth had never before opened it. Now she heard his firm footsteps crossing his bedroom, and the door closing behind him as he went out into the corridor.

She turned back then to the square silver box, inserted the tiny key in the lock, and lifted back the lid.

"Oh," she said softly. "Oh!" She could not find any words adequate to express her wonder and delight. Diamonds, pearls, emeralds, sapphires, necklaces, bracelets, rings, earrings— the Garth jewel collection was spread before her, catching and reflecting a thousand lights.

One by one she held them up, tried them on. At length, with shaking fingers, she adjusted the catch on a necklace of emeralds, hung emerald pendants in her ears, and with a final look at herself in the mirror, she followed Don down the stairs.

He and Terry were talking and laughing with an easy companionship that made her feel left out. Terry had long been a deep and fervent admirer of Don's and his feeling for

20

the older man had only been strengthened when the latter had married his only sister.

They broke off their conversation and rose to their feet as she entered the drawing room. Terry's lips puckered in a whistle. "Here comes the bride!"

Instinctively Penny looked at Don from under her long lashes. The smile had frozen on his lips. His eyes met hers searchingly, intently, for a moment, as though seeking the answer to a question. Something had leaped into them that she had not seen since the moment she started down the church aisle toward him in her wedding dress. Then his eyes were veiled and he was holding a chair for her, his face blank.

"Penny," her brother exclaimed. "Those emeralds—can they possibly be real?"

"The bridegroom's present to his bride," Don said without any expression in his voice.

The boy drew a long breath. "I'd heard of the Garth jewel collection," he said, awed. "But I had no idea they were as lovely as that. Such incredible green, Penny! And stunning with your coloring."

Would Don say they were becoming? Penny waited breathlessly.

"Glad you found something to go with that yellow dress," he said.

"Oh, Don," she exclaimed, "I've never seen anything like them! Never in my life. I could spend hours just looking at them, touching them. But are they safe here?"

"I have a—" Don broke off as Fane appeared in the doorway to announce, "Dinner is served."

Don, Penny realized, was as aware of the difference made by Terry's presence as she was. For the first time since their wedding, dinner passed in a spate of gay talk, filled with laughter, without long pauses. Several times she was aware that her brother was giving her quick glances. What was he looking at? But it was not until Fane and the waitress had withdrawn that he leaned forward and touched his sister's arm with a gentle finger.

"What happened to our Lucky Penny? Looks to me as though someone had grabbed her and given her a shake. Are there black and blue spots on the other arm, too?"

"Don't be silly," Penny said. She could feel herself coloring fiercely. "You know how easily I bruise and how long the bruises last. That was—that was Nora when she grabbed

21

hold of me for a last embrace before—before Don and I left for our—wedding trip."

Terry laughed, reassured. "Poor Nora! She doesn't know her own strength. When do you expect her at Uplands?"

"She's coming tomorrow, bag and baggage." Penny gave a mock sigh. "And from now on I shan't be able to call my soul my own."

Any suspicion that might have touched Terry's mind in regard to the bruises on Penny's arms faded away and she steeled herself to meet Don's eyes as she rose from the table. His face was so white that it shocked her. She wanted to cry out: It doesn't matter. You didn't hurt me. Don't look like that. But she could not do it before Terry.

Later, she thought. I'll find a chance to tell him later. But when she and Terry were settled in the drawing room Don excused himself.

"Sorry to leave you on your first evening at home," he said, and Terry flushed with pleasure at the genuine welcome in his brother-in-law's voice. "But I'm swamped with work. Can't seem to catch up."

"Ye gods, work on a honeymoon?" Terry said incredulously.

For several hours Penelope played cards with Terry. At last he declared that he was all in and went off whistling to bed. The girl waited till she heard his door close with a mighty bang before she entered the great hall with its rare, soft rugs and dark oak paneling. There was a light under the door of Don's study. He was still up. She drew a sigh of relief. Then something, a faint movement, caught her attention. At her left was the dining room. On the far side, facing the door, was a buffet with a long mirror behind it. The dining room was dimly lighted from a single wall bracket. In the mirror she caught another flicker of movement and stood watching.

She moved forward a cautious step, her footfall deadened by the heavy rug. Fane was reflected in the mirror. He was looking down intently at something in his hand. Penny took another step. The thing in the butler's hand was a small revolver and he was busily engaged in loading it.

IV

For a moment Penelope was too surprised to move. Fane loading a revolver! Why? The country place at Uplands was isolated but it was well guarded and there were a number of servants. Had the butler taken on himself the extra job of watchdog? Or was he arming himself for some other purpose?

His intentness, his secrecy, loading the gun in the dining room, out of sight of the other servants, all indicated that he wanted no one to know what he was doing. I'll have to tell Don, the girl decided. She sighed. Poor Don! All I bring him is worry.

She thought of his cordial kindness to her brother that evening, his warm invitation to make Uplands his home, his lighthearted chatter that had made him look so much younger, almost as young as Terry himself. But when he had turned to her the laughter had faded, he had become once more the coldly polite stranger.

Except, Penny thought, when he saw the bruises on her arms, the bruises he had made, and realized what he had done. He had been so white that it had frightened her. She must reassure him.

She stood with one slender hand on the door of Don's study. When he was not at the Works he continued to be busy in the study, whose door had always been closed to her. In his rare free moments he dropped in at Geoffrey Jarvis's cottage. Penny wondered a little at the friendship between two men who were so different in character: Don carrying the weight of responsibility for the Works, Geoff a playboy who seemed to take nothing seriously but parties, polo and yachting.

Unexpectedly, she found that she was shy of demanding entrance to the study. At length she turned with a swirl of yellow skirts and ran up the stairs. She removed the emerald necklace and the earrings, locked them into the silver jewel box and, holding it in both hands, retraced her steps to the study.

She took a deep breath, lifted her chin and tapped lightly at the door. Don opened it and looked at her in surprise.

Then his eyes went down to the silver box in her hands and his jaw tightened.

"Please," she began, feeling her courage slip away, "please, may I come in for a moment?"

He stood back to let her pass him and then closed the door behind her.

"Won't you sit down?" he asked formally as he drew a chair near his table desk.

Penelope sank into it with a little shiver at the detached civility of his tone. To gain time she looked around the room. It was paneled to the ceiling in richly colored wood. Bookshelves lined one wall. A massive built-in safe was on one side of the fireplace. The desk was piled high with papers. The only jarring note was Don's desk chair, a heavy ornate affair, upholstered in leather and too elaborately decorated with its knobs and furbelows.

Between two doors hung a fine portrait of the founder of the Works and below it were pictures showing the development of the business from the shacklike hut in which the first wagon had been built to the great buildings in which automobiles had been made, and finally the industrial city with its streets of buildings, in which the fastest and most efficient airplanes in America were being produced.

A portrait of Donald's mother was set like a medallion into the dark wood above the mantel. Its beauty and color glowed like a gem in the somber setting. What a characteristic room it was, characteristic of the man who occupied it. She had not entered it since her marriage.

She looked up at the man who had so sternly set her outside his life. He stood behind his desk gravely waiting for her to speak. She saw his jaw tighten as his eyes rested for a moment on the bruises on her arms. They came back to her face.

"What is it, Penelope?"

She gave a nervous ripple of laughter. "First—won't you please sit down? You are so—so forbidding looming over me like that."

He sat down, rapped the ashes from his pipe and laid it on his desk. She clasped her hands around the heavy silver box and leaned toward him, her shining eyes on his, her vivid lips parted. Each tiny fleck of gold on her dress glimmered like a spark under the light of the desk lamp. She was vibrant with youth and beauty and eagerness.

For a moment Don looked at her with an answering eagerness and then he kept his eyes steadily on the pliable ivory

24

letter opener he was bending back and forth between his lean, strong fingers.

She laid the jewel box on the desk. "I'm afraid to keep it in my room," she said. "I've never seen anything so magnificent as those diamonds and emeralds. They must be worth a fortune. Suppose something should happen to them. To-night you started to say, 'I have a—' and stopped when Fane came to announce dinner. I thought perhaps you were going to say that you have a safe and I see—" she looked at the heavy wall safe—"that you have. Will you keep the box here?"

"If you will promise to wear the jewelry," he said.

"I'll love wearing it," she exclaimed. "Don, there's something else, so much else I want to say to you. First, I want to thank you for making Terry feel so at home here."

"Penelope," he said quietly, "do you—do you feel at all at home at Uplands?"

"I love it," she said warmly. "It's beautiful, it has dignity and tradition. Only—"

"Only what?"

"Don't snap at me," she said with an unsteady laugh. "Only I want to be busy. There's no—place for me here. I mean," she went on before he could speak, "I'm not really needed. The housekeeper does everything. I want to be busy, Don, terribly busy, with something really important to do." There was a break in her voice.

"You don't want time to think, is that it?" Don added savagely, "Do you still care that much for Wentworth?" The ivory paper opener snapped in pieces and he flung it on the desk.

"Don," she half cried out, stretching her hands toward his in pleading. "That's not it. Really, really, that's not it." She gathered her thoughts together and told him of the tentative plans she had made that afternoon to make the village a better place to live in, to help build good citizens for the future.

"I believe I could do it," she said earnestly, "and I am sure that it is worth doing."

"Do you realize how much work it would entail?" he asked her. "How many hours, how much thought, how much planning?"

She nodded. "But it would be worth it. There are a number of women I could enlist to help me and perhaps some of the men at the Works would volunteer to assist with the plans for adolescent boys, entertaining them, instructing them in something—"

"It's a magnificent idea," he said slowly. "With your enthusiasm I believe you'll make a success of it. I wish you luck." He added, "And it would build good will for the Works to have the employees realize that my wife is doing so much for them."

"Oh, I hoped it would," she said softly, her eyes shining.

"Do you mean that?" he asked huskily. He got up so quickly that his awkward, massive desk chair swung around. "Pen—those marks on your arm—did I make them that day when we—" His voice failed him.

Her light laugh held a strain of emotion. "That's really why I wanted to see you, Don. When Terry noticed them I saw your face. I wanted to tell you that I wasn't hurt, that it didn't matter, that—anyhow—" her voice was unsteady and she had difficulty in controlling it—"anyhow, I didn't blame you. I deserved—"

In one stride he was beside her. He bent suddenly and pressed his lips to the soft, bruised flesh. Penelope's heart leaped into her throat. She looked down at the dark head so close to her own. She felt an almost overwhelming impulse to press her cheek against his own, to whisper to him that it was all right, everything was all right. To comfort him for his self-reproach at hurting her.

"Do you mean it, Pen? Do you mean it, my darling?" he said huskily. He lifted his head.

There was a tap at the door and he moved away from her. "Come in," he called.

Fane came into the room bearing a letter on a silver tray. Don took it from him and the butler went out. Penelope watched him go, the platelike face serene, eyes blank, the perfectly trained servant who sees nothing but what he is permitted to see. No one would think that a few moments before he had been surreptitiously loading a gun. I must tell Don, Penelope thought. Something happened to me when I came into this room. I forgot to tell him. But I must do it now.

She looked up with a half smile that faded when she saw his face, hard and white and set.

"This is for you, I believe," he said with frigid courtesy.

In surprise and consternation at the change in him, she took the letter he held out to her. She recognized the sprawling, undisciplined handwriting. It was from Dick Wentworth.

"Don," she cried out in sharp protest at what she saw in his eyes. "Don, I never gave Dick permission to write to me. I know I've been a failure as a wife but I—you can trust me, Don."

26

He looked down at her, studying her face. Why, oh, why couldn't he believe her? she thought. She should have told him how her feelings had changed for Dick, that she no longer loved him. She owed that much to her husband. She had not spoken before because it humiliated her to think how mistaken she had been, that she had spoiled Don's life for the sake of a man like Dick. And then—then, since their marriage, her husband had offered no opportunities for confidences. It was too late. He no longer cared whom she loved.

Slowly his cold eyes warmed, a smile touched them and moved to his lips. Before he could speak, the telephone on the desk rang sharply.

Don picked it up. "Yes? . . . Washington? All right. Go ahead."

The watching girl saw his face light up, warm with pleasure. "Kitty!" he exclaimed. "It's wonderful to hear from you." He listened, smiling. Then he laughed outright. "You haven't changed at all. . . ."

Penelope waited irresolutely. Should she go? Don seemed to have forgotten that she was in the room, that she was in the world. It made her feel very lonely and remote from his interests.

He went on talking, laughing with boyish amusement. How long was it since he had laughed like that with her? Not since their marriage. Who was this Kitty whose call entertained him so much? She had never heard him mention a girl named Kitty.

And then his eyes flashed to her face. She saw them widen with incredulous amazement, then flame with a light she couldn't understand. She got to her feet and went toward the door, unaware that her mouth was drooping, her head was down. She waved her hand to indicate that she would leave him to carry on his conversation in privacy.

Absently he nodded his head and returned with renewed animation to his talk with the woman he had called, with so much pleasure, Kitty.

Passionately angry, heart and brain in a tumult of humiliation, Penelope went out, closing the door behind her with a sharp little bang which somewhat relieved her feelings. She ran up the stairs and along the corridor to her suite of rooms. Her cheeks burned, her eyes were wide and hot as she paced back and forth in her pretty sitting room. Don had let her go as though she were in the way, only a troublesome child.

Who was Kitty? Who was this woman to whom he talked with a warmth, a pleasure he never showed in talking to her?

27

For a moment he had seemed very close. Through her whole body she could feel the thrill when his lips had touched her arm. He had almost seemed to forgive her. In another moment she would have explained how her feelings had changed for Dick. And then the butler had come in with that letter and the mood of the moment had been shattered.

The letter! She had forgotten it. Why had Dick written to her? She had made clear to him that they were never to meet again, that her love for him was dead, that she would be loyal to Don.

Did he think that she would change her mind? Did he believe she still loved him? In a way, she could hardly blame him—the change had come so quickly. He must think she would still answer when he called, that marriage meant nothing to her.

She tore open the letter which she still held in her hand. *Penelope, my dearest,* it began.

No, she rebelled. He has no right. She crushed the letter in her hand and flung it into the wastebasket. But a woman's curiosity is too strong. She dug it out again, smoothed the crumpled pages.

Penelope, my dearest—for you will always be my dearest. When I tried to talk to you that last time, on your wedding day, I felt that you had misunderstood me, that things were wrong between us. I'll always love you and you will always love me. I know why you had to marry Garth and I would have prevented it if I could. You know that. It has been a nightmare, thinking of the sacrifice you had to make. But no mistake is irrevocable, Penny. We belong together. Let me see you—talk to you—and we will be able to make plans for a bright new future. Send me a word and I will know that you are willing to hear what I have to say. Always your Dick.

She flung the sheet of paper down on a low table. How outrageous of Dick! Did he believe for a single minute that, when she had taken her marriage vows, she would see him, listen to him? Love? That was not love, not love as she believed it would be. There could be no love without complete trust. She did not trust him. She knew it now. And he had no faith, no understanding of her integrity, to have written as he did.

She went into her bedroom and, standing before her dressing table, removed the dress she had put on with such pleasure

28

a few hours earlier, slipping into a white velvet robe which had been a part of her trousseau. She began to brush her hair furiously. It waved away from her face in dusky, satiny softness. Her cheeks were flushed, her eyes brilliant with indignation.

Oddly enough, the indignation had little to do with Dick and the letter she had almost forgotten. Kitty, she thought to herself wrathfully. I can just picture her, a fluffy white angora kitten—with claws. And fair probably, blond and pink and white. Not a dark gypsy like you.

She looked at her dark hair and eyes, at her vivid coloring of cheeks and lips, with ineffable scorn. Everyone prefers blondes, she told herself. She pulled the brush through her hair so viciously that it brought tears to her eyes.

There was a tap on the door of her sitting room. In answer to her call Don came in. He saw her at her dressing table and stood where he was, in the middle of the sitting room, beside the low table on which Dick's letter lay with its big sprawling writing.

For a moment he stood stock-still. Penelope, knowing that the letter could be read almost in one swift glance, was rigid. If he would only say something, show that he really believed in her—

He stood looking at her and his face revealed nothing at all. His hands were thrust deep into the pockets of his impeccable dinner jacket.

"Sorry I had to break up our little talk," he said easily. "That was a telephone call from an old friend of mine. She has just returned to this country after living for some time in England, where her husband died. Her home in Washington is being redecorated and she has no place to stay. Will you please write and ask her to visit us at Uplands while her own place is being put in shape for her?"

"Of course," Penelope said steadily. She went out to the sitting room, the white velvet robe trailing behind her. She sat down at her small inlaid desk. "What is the address?"

"Mrs. Thomas Scarlet," he said. He handed her a slip of paper. "This is the address. Oh, and it would be nice to ask her mother to come, too—Mrs. Hamilton Owens. You don't mind?"

"Why should I? You have a right to entertain your friends in your own house."

"Yes." He glanced down at the discarded letter and the words died in his throat. "You seem—you seem comfortable here. You—you look very lovely in that white robe. The

29

velvet is like your skin." He turned abruptly toward the door. "Good night, Pen."

Pen! The girl stared at the door as it closed behind Donald Garth. It was the first time he had called her Pen since— since— She controlled a mad impulse to rush after him and demand, beg if necessary, that he forgive her and take her back into his friendship. She paused with her hand on the doorknob. What good would it do? He did not care for her any more. And Kitty was coming.

She stood looking down at the address written in Don's clear hand. Who, she wondered, was Kitty Scarlet?

ii

Donald Garth closed the door of Penny's sitting room behind him and went back downstairs to his study. The silver box still lay on his desk where she had left it. He remembered the emerald necklace and the earrings against her sun-tanned skin, setting off the soft yellow of her dress. How lovely she was!

He closed and locked the door, saw that the draperies covering the windows and the French doors that opened onto the garden were drawn, before he put the jewel casket away.

He settled himself in the big desk chair and drew toward him a stack of papers, but his mind was not on them. He thought of Penny's arm, silken smooth, when his mouth had touched the faint blue mark made by his fingers during that convulsive moment of rage that had followed the revelation of her true reason for marrying him.

Skin like velvet indeed. No wonder he had fled from her after speaking the words. Sometimes it seemed to him that the iron control he had demanded of himself would be bound to give way some day when she leaned toward him as she had tonight in his study, her eyes shining, so lovely, so lovely.

He hoped that he would never again suffer as he had suffered when he had overheard Nora tell Penny that Dick Wentworth was waiting to see her and had listened to Penny's confession. The girl he had loved so deeply had married him for his money, loving another man!

In the weeks since his marriage he had followed his plan faithfully. He asked nothing of her. He had maintained a careful, impersonal balance. He wanted nothing of her that she would not be willing to give with her whole heart. He was willing to wait.

30

And now Dick Wentworth had written, secure in her love, expecting that she would be willing to receive him at Uplands. Surely she would not agree. And yet—what did he know about her, after all? Except that he loved her. That he would always love her.

He bent over the papers, moving the telephone out of his way. The sight of it reminded him of Kitty Scarlet's call and her request that she let her make a visit to Uplands. A light kindled at the back of his eyes and grew to a flame. It touched his mouth and curved the stern lips in a delighted smile. Kitty, he thought in satisfaction.

V

Penelope resembled nothing so much as a gigantic pink peony as she knelt before one of the garden beds at Uplands some time later. With deft fingers she was attacking the weeds. If she could not be the wife Don wanted and deserved, at least she could make his garden bloom, make his house warm and attractive for him and for his guests.

The word guest reminded her of the unknown Kitty, who was to descend upon them and who had written a letter of eager, almost gushing acceptance to Penny's invitation. Penny felt as though something were squeezing her heart when she thought of Kitty Scarlet and remembered her husband's voice when he had spoken to the unknown woman on the telephone.

"Mary, Mary, quite contrary, how does your garden grow?" called a voice from the top of the low wall which enclosed the garden.

"Geoffrey Jarvis! However did you get there without my hearing you?" the girl cried.

She dropped trowel and weeder and, with a sigh of relief, settled back on her heels to contemplate the lean, good-humored face of the man above her. His clear blue eyes were heavily shaded by black lashes, his features were finely modeled, his dark hair left the top of his head somewhat perilously exposed to wind and weather, his skin was dark and clear; the man gave an impression of wholesome soundness.

Her first sight of Jarvis always surprised Penny. He had the air of a man of purpose, a man who was devoting his energies to carrying out important missions, and yet his was the reputation of a playboy, an idle fellow who spent his time

31

giving and going to parties, playing polo, sailing in his yacht. Once more she was struck by the contrast between his life and that of Garth, who was his closest friend. And yet, when she was with Jarvis, met his steady eyes, the friendship seemed not only natural but inevitable.

He returned her scrutiny with interest. The May sun shone upon her uncovered hair. It transmuted the ends of rebellious tendrils to glinting bronze. Her clear skin was lightly flushed, her eyes were soft and deep. The red of her lips was curved in laughter, two deep dimples indented her cheeks. He concealed his admiration beneath a sort of big-brother banter.

"Why are you digging, Penny? Has Garth given up his gardeners?"

"Most of the available men around here are employed at the Works now. Anyhow, I love doing this. We need something beautiful to look at, don't we? One may not live by bread alone, you know. In this troubled world we need all the color and fragrance of flowers."

He cleared his throat sharply as he looked at the lovely face with the touch of pathos about the curved lips.

"Look here," he laughed, "you may be turning out a prize-winning garden, but you are playing the deuce with that skin of yours. Your nose resembles the taillight on an automobile and your throat—an Indian in full war paint would look anemic beside you."

She favored him with a laughing grimace.

"If you continue to pay me such fulsome compliments, Mr. Jarvis, I shall burst with vanity. And what are you doing around here at the ungodly hour of nine in the morning? I thought you never got up before noon."

"That," he declared with pretended anger, "is sheer slander. I'm a very energetic man."

"You!" she exclaimed mockingly. "What on earth do you do with all your energy when you aren't playing polo?"

He gave her a queer glance but he answered laughingly, "I invent new salads for dinner. Very important, that. I plan new voyages for the yacht. I loaf and invite my soul."

He lighted a cigarette and contemplated her, smiling. "Of course, that doesn't sound like a busy life to a demon of energy like you. The village is buzzing with talk about the projects you are working out: nursery schools, playgrounds, heaven knows what all. You've become a heroine. If Don doesn't look out, you'll be his rival for the love of this community."

He sobered. "By the way, where is Don?"

"At the Works, I suppose," she said in surprise. "He seems to leave earlier and earlier."

A frown touched Jarvis's insouciant face and was immediately smoothed away. "No," he said lightly, "he's not there. Doesn't seem to have put in an appearance yet. Thought I'd drop by and see if he was still here." He dropped off the wall. "I'll be looking forward to seeing what you do with that garden and with all your other projects, Penny."

She looked up in surprise. "You aren't going so soon!"

"I think I'll drive down to the Works. Just to make sure Don got there." He laughed but his eyes were shadowed with anxiety.

When he had gone Penny still crouched on her heels beside the flower bed, staring unseeingly at the ground. It was ridiculous to think that Geoffrey Jarvis was worried about Don. There was nothing to worry about. And Geoffrey never took anything seriously.

She reached for the trowel. In her ears were the words, *Just to make sure Don got there.* Why shouldn't he get there? Don wasn't in any danger. Nothing could hap—

She got up abruptly, pulling off her gardening gloves. For some reason, which she did not in the least understand, she felt a sudden need to be sure that Don was all right. Ridiculous, she told herself. Nonetheless, the feeling hung on, grew more persistent. She turned on her heel, went into the house and up to her suite.

She pulled off her gardening clothes and dressed in a simple, soft green suit and a crisp blouse. She reached for gloves and handbag.

A few minutes later, at the wheel of the cream-colored convertible which Don always left at Uplands for her own use, she was rolling toward the Works, still puzzled, still confused by the instinct within her which was forcing her on.

As she came in sight of the great airplane plant she slowed down and finally stopped the car, gazing ahead of her at the acres of buildings enclosed within substantial iron railings. She had never been inside the place which occupied so much of her husband's attention. For a moment she felt a thrill of pride at what the Garth family had achieved.

Once there had been nothing but a barnlike building in which Don's grandfather had built wagons. With the advent of the automobile the buildings and the business had grown with mushroom speed. Today, the city of great buildings was devoted to the construction of airplanes. The Garth Airplane

33

Works, she thought with a thrill of pride, represented, symbolized, the forward march of America itself. She could hear the ceaseless whirr of belts, the hum of countless wheels, could sense the feverish, purposeful activity within.

She sat at the wheel in an agony of uncertainty. Never before had she gone farther than the massive gates. How was she to explain her presence there? Perhaps Don would be annoyed at having her come. She started the motor, was about to turn around and go back, but the curious uncertainty that had brought her here would not allow her to turn back. She drove up to the gates.

The guard recognized her, the gate swung open. "Good morning, Mrs. Garth."

She smiled at him. "Where can I find Mr. Garth?"

He pointed out the way across the quadrangle to the entrance to the office building. Penny parked the convertible and went inside. At the reception desk a trim-looking girl with a pleasant face looked at her admiringly.

"I am Mrs. Garth. Is my husband at leisure?"

The girl smiled. "Good morning, Mrs. Garth. Mr. Garth," and she shook her head, "is never at leisure. But I know he'll have time for you."

She spoke over the telephone and in a few moments another alert-looking young woman came down the hall.

"Mrs. Garth?" she said. "I am Helen Travis, Mr. Garth's secretary. Will you come this way, please?"

As Penny accompanied her down a long corridor the secretary said, "You have no idea how excited people are about your plans for the village. The homemaking course! I could go for that myself."

She led the way into a big office with windows on two sides. Garth, sitting at a huge desk, pushed aside papers and got to his feet as she came in.

Penny was aware of an overwhelming sense of relief. Don was there. He was all right. Although, what could have happened to him she did not know. She must have been crazy to become so alarmed by a laughing comment from Jarvis, a passing frown on his face. Nevertheless, she was almost limp with the release of her worry.

Don stood waiting courteously for her to speak.

"I—I hope you don't mind," she stammered. "I—you know I've never really seen the Works. I wondered—"

For a moment his eyes searched her face keenly. "Of course," he said, "I'll get someone to take you through." He pressed a button. When his secretary came in, he said, "Miss

Travis, will you get hold of McGregor and tell him I'd appreciate it if he'd take my wife through the Works."

Miss Travis laughed. "If the employees find out who Mrs. Garth is, he'll need a guard. She'll be mobbed. About all they talk of these days is her plans for the village and making life better for them and their children."

When she had gone out, Don held a chair for Penny, but she went to look out of one of the windows. "I didn't know it was like this," she said, fascinated by the sight and sound of so much purposeful activity.

Garth stood beside her. His eyes were glowing, his face more alive than it usually was when he spoke to her. "We are doing big work here," he said, "important work not only for industry, nor even for the country as a whole, but—" He checked himself. "I'm—proud of the Works, Penelope, and proud of what my family has accomplished."

"But you—everyone says you have done miracles here yourself, Don."

He turned to her but before he could answer the door opened and a rosy-faced Scot in his early sixties came into the office.

A smile glimmered in his colorless eyes as he acknowledged Garth's introduction. "Of course, I have time to take Mrs. Garth through," he answered promptly in response to his employer's question.

Looking back at the window, Penelope was conscious that Garth watched them for several minutes before he turned back to his desk. She heard a steel door clang and then promptly forgot him in her interest in what was before her. A city of industry lay behind those iron railings. Blocks of buildings and a series of factories stretched out interminably.

"I hope," Penny said to the Scot, "I am not taking up too much of your time."

He gave her a slow smile. "There would always be time for you, Mrs. Garth. My grandfather worked for Mr. Garth's grandfather, and the McGregors have been working here ever since. My son is chief accountant and my grandson—" He broke off, his face shadowed.

"What you're planning to do about playgrounds and keeping an eye on the adolescent boys—it's going to mean a lot, Mrs. Garth. My grandson's been getting wild, out of hand, because he hasn't enough to occupy his leisure time, give him a purpose. You're going to help boys like that."

"I'm terribly glad," Penny said softly. "I want to help."

He nodded. "I could have told that when I first looked at

you," he said gruffly. "Like Mr. Garth, you are. I'm glad for him he's got such a wife. He deserves the best there is, and I guess he's got it."

Penny's throat tightened. If he only knew! McGregor walked at her side, pointing out the various operations, explaining what was being done and how it was being handled. There were, Penny realized, literally tens of thousands of employees for whom Donald Garth was responsible, men for whom the Works provided employment; and beyond them, their families, wives and children, for whom the employment meant food and housing and education. No wonder Don worked so hard, no wonder he looked so tired. He had carried this responsibility almost from the time he had left college.

Penelope's guide hurried her through shop after shop until she had a confused sense of whirling belts and wheels, rasping files and ringing hammers and noise —always incessant noise. She gave a little sigh of relief when she reached the cool, cloistered stillness of the emergency wards, where she talked for a moment to a smiling, capable, white-clad nurse.

She was turning to leave when the door opened and Garth came in. The nurse brightened.

"Only a few accidents today," she said, "and no serious injuries."

Garth nodded and went into the room beyond with its row of white beds.

"He comes every day," the nurse told Penny, "and always takes time, no matter how busy he is, to talk to the men. No wonder they think so much of him."

When Garth came out he raised his brows. "Have you seen enough?" he asked.

"Enough! Are you hoping that I shall say yes?" she challenged. "Because if you are, you will be horribly disappointed. I think this is the most wonderful place. I should love to work here."

"Perhaps you'd like to see the rest some other time. The din is maddening, deafening to anyone who is not accustomed to it."

"Oh, Don, please!" she implored him. "I'm not tired. I'm simply dazed by the magnitude of the work you are doing."

"Come on then. Watch your step. Thanks, McGregor. I'll show my wife the rest of it." He turned to Penny. "I'll give you a little rest from the noise."

He led her into a big room, which seemed to be all windows, where men were bending over blueprints. Something about one of the draftsmen made Penny stop to watch. His lean sinewy hands were vibrant with energy. He looked up suddenly at the vivid, earnest face of the girl. His eyes, which seemed to flame into red lights, swept to the man behind her before they dropped to his work.

In that instant his face had been indelibly photographed on Penelope's mind. She shivered. It was such a young face to be so tragic and his eyes—his eyes had been like those of a hungry wolf. She looked from him to the mammoth flag of the Stars and Stripes which hung almost over his head— and wondered. She gave an unconscious sigh of relief as she followed Garth into the open air and across the quadrangle to where the cream-colored convertible was waiting.

"What is over there?" she asked as she indicated a group of buildings which stood apart and were heavily guarded.

There was a little pause and then Garth said, "Just at present I can't answer that question."

"I understand. Thank you, Don, for letting me see all this. It is inspiring." Her eyes rested for a moment on the heavily guarded buildings. "How," she asked, "if you have hundreds of men working there, can you keep your secret—whatever it is?"

His eyes narrowed in frowning thoughtfulness.

"The majority are honest and earnest. There are some—" He shrugged away his seriousness. "Well, the others get our undivided attention. Anyhow, our chief security rests in the fact that only one man is familiar with the whole picture."

The guard rolled back the great gates and closed them behind Penny with a respectful, "Good morning, Mrs. Garth." Behind her a siren screamed out, telling the men that it was time for lunch.

VI

Petro bent over the blueprints, blinking to clear his tired, blurred eyes. They were tired because he had not slept. All night he had tossed, hearing in his mind the low words of the man who had befriended him, got him this job he loved, the man to whom he owed everything.

Everything? No, he told himself fiercely, not everything. He owed much to this new land of his. All through his frightened childhood in war-torn Europe he had dreamed of America, of living in a country where men walked unafraid, where he could do the work of which he dreamed, designing airplanes that could go faster and higher than planes had ever gone before.

Through the help of an American who had learned of his ability he had had a totally unexpected, unhoped-for opportunity to enter the United States. He had escaped from terror and slavery to hope and freedom, promising his young brothers and sisters that as soon as he could provide for them, they were to join him.

And now that he had been admitted, that he had taken out —so proudly—his first papers, that he was preparing to become a citizen, he wanted to believe that America was not the only giver; that he, too, had something to contribute to his new country.

Through the same American, he had attained his job at the Garth Airplane Works and he was happy for the first time in his young life. The American had been more than a benefactor. He had become a friend to whom Petro owed a debt too great to repay.

Then, last night, his friend had come to see him, a friend so changed that he hardly recognized him. The pleasant smile was gone, the eyes were as hard as bullets. In short, ugly phrases he had told Petro what he expected of him.

The vital, energetic young hands had been flung out in wild protest. "But I can't do that," he said. "I cannot give you any information about the new plane."

The man who had been his friend smiled then, but there was no mirth in his smile. This was not a request, he explained. It was an order. He must have the information and he must have it at once. Otherwise, and the smile grew deeper, more frightening, otherwise something rather—unpleasant —would happen to Petro's young brothers and sisters, who still lived in their own country, without anyone to protect them.

The man who had become a hostile stranger waited patiently for Petro to grasp all the ugly implications of his threat. He saw the boy grow haggard as he thought of the harmless, innocent youngsters, of what would happen to them if he failed.

Petro had seen other people disappear in a night, he had seen the bodies of children who had been killed in horrible ways. He held his head in his hands, moaning.

At last, white-faced and shaking, he explained. "Even if— even if I wanted to do this thing," he said, "I cannot. It is out of my power. Each department at the plant knows a little, a very little. It is like a—jigsaw puzzle. We each have a piece. But we do not know where our piece fits in; we do not know what the whole picture is like. Only Mr. Garth knows it all."

For a long time the man who had been his friend studied his face, searching it. And he knew, at length, that Petro had told him the truth. He walked up and down Petro's small bedroom in the boardinghouse where he lived, kicking savagely at a chair in his way. At last, he had turned around.

"Then," he said, "we have two choices. We'll tear the Works apart, if necessary, to find where the blueprints are concealed. If we fail at that—Garth must talk."

"He will never talk," Petro said quickly. "Never in the world."

"He can be made to talk," the man said with a bitter twist to his lips. "There are ways."

Petro, seeing the man's expression, hearing his voice, began to shake.

"What—what will you do to him?" he asked hoarsely. "He has been very good to me."

The other man laughed. "We'll take care of that. Bring him to me. I don't care how you do it. Kidnap him, knock him out, trick him into coming. There are a hundred ways. But bring him alive. I'll handle the rest." Again the smile touched his mouth. "And he'll talk."

Petro blinked his eyes again and bent over the blueprints. Mr. Garth would talk. There were limits beyond which no man could bear pain. Petro as a boy had heard the screams of strong men when the agony of torture became more than they could bear, heard them cry out the secrets they meant to keep because they were no longer in control of their will.

Someone stopped near him and he looked up to see a girl watching him with wide friendly eyes. She was, he thought, the loveliest thing he had ever seen. Behind her stood Donald Garth, the head of the Works—the man whom he must, in one way or another, take to the man with the smiling face and the cruel eyes, unless the blueprints were found at the Works.

Petro looked down, his vivid imagination picturing the fine face above him distorted with agony, the firm mouth gaping with a terrible scream, the beautifully shaped hands torn and twisted by torture.

When he looked up again the couple had gone. A flicker of color caught his eyes, the Stars and Stripes hanging over his head. He looked up at it for a long time. Those stars were

39

not set there by accident. Each one meant a state carved out of virgin forest, in baking heat and freezing cold, by men who had bridged great rivers and tunneled through mountains and built a land up step by step with infinite labor and with faith in the future. This flag was the symbol of what those men had achieved.

At last, through his confusion and turmoil, he heard the noon siren. He got up, swaying a little dizzily, and left the table.

ii

A yelp at the side of the road brought Penny back to her surroundings. She peered into the bushes. Huddled in a dejected heap lay a dog. His tail thumped frantically as she jumped from her car and knelt beside him, heedless of her trim suit; his big brown eyes met hers pleadingly. He licked her hands with his rough tongue as she gently took his bruised leg between her fingers. She patted his head.

He had been run over by a motorist who had not bothered to stop.

"Good old dog," she said quietly. "Let me look. I won't hurt you."

With a yelp of pain the dog tried to extricate its injured leg from her firm but gentle grip. "Nice boy," she said soothingly.

She looked at him in perplexity and then, with an effort, lifted him and made her somewhat staggering way back to the car. She was so absorbed in the injured dog as she laid it on the seat beside her that she did not hear a strangled cry from behind the car.

When she reached Uplands she drove around to the garage where the chauffeur, with an exclamation of surprise, came running and took the dog from her arms. At her instructions he made a bed of clean straw for her patient, where the dog lay on its side like a baby, brown eyes intent on the girl's deft fingers, as she bandaged the injured leg. The tail thumped spasmodically.

"What kind of dog is he, Hawkins?" she asked, as she regarded her salvage work speculatively.

The man, who had grown old and bent in the service of the Garths, added another furrow to the collection which the years had etched on his brow.

"I'm jiggered if I know, ma'am. First I think he's a pointer,

40

then I see a bit of hound, and I'll be beat if he hasn't got a head like a setter—"

The girl sank down on the ground beside the dog, with a little ripple of laughter. The sound stopped in her throat as she heard running feet come up the driveway and a young man stopped beside her, his chest rising and falling with his panting breath. It was the young man she had seen bending over a blueprint at the Works.

He dropped down beside her and the dog began to yelp with delight, lavishing caresses with his red tongue on the face that bent over him. The man took the dog in his arms.

Penny smiled sympathetically. "It isn't necessary to ask if that is your dog."

At the sound of the girl's voice the young man sprang to his feet. The expression in the eyes that had been so stricken was now quite different. They held a look of mingled yearning and hopelessness.

"Didn't I see you at the Works this morning?" Penny asked.

He stiffened. "Yes, ma'am."

"And this, I can see, is your dog."

"Yes, ma'am, Vag's mine. My friend—my family—all I've got. Usually he waits for me outside the Works but when I got out, I saw you picking him up. I—ran all the way."

He shifted his cap in the nervous fingers Penelope remembered so well. She looked at him thoughtfully. His was not the voice of the usual workman. It was educated, cultivated, with a faint hint of accent which she could not place.

"I am glad that I found him." The warm friendliness of the girl's tone sent a red tide to the man's brow. "But I think you'd better not try to move him now. Let me keep him for a week. I'll promise to take good care of him. Of course, come to see him whenever you like. Hawkins, be sure this young man is admitted to see his dog."

"I thank you, ma'am, I thank you."

"That's all right."

"And I'll be back to see Vag—short for Vagabond."

"What is your name?"

"Petro, ma'am."

Penny straightened up and gave some instructions to Hawkins about calling a veterinary. "He'll be better here where he is taken care of than left alone while you are working, Petro," she explained. Then, with a smiling nod to the young man, she turned toward the house.

As she did so, she caught her breath. Startled. Fane was

41

so close behind her that she had nearly stepped on him. The butler moved away with a hasty apology but his eyes never left the face of the young draftsman until, after a prolonged farewell with his dog, Petro turned and went back down the driveway.

VII

Several days later, Penny straightened up from gardening, looked over the results of her handiwork with satisfaction, and turned back to the house.

Someone was crawling along the driveway, his clothes muddy and torn, a tiny rivulet of blood trickling down one cheek. He tried to lift himself and then collapsed and lay face down on the gravel.

Penny ran madly toward him. Bent over. It was Geoffrey Jarvis, lying unconscious, his face ghastly. His leg was twisted at an unnatural angle. It must be broken. How far had he crawled in that terrible condition?

At her cry of horror, people came running. Fane and Don's man, Macy, lifted the unconscious Jarvis between them, carried him into the house and up to a guest room while a maid prepared the bed and Penny telephoned for a doctor.

Sometime later, the doctor came down to her where she waited tensely in the small morning room at the back of the house overlooking the gardens. Here she worked on her plans for the village projects but now she could only wait, wondering what had happened to Jarvis, how badly he had been hurt, and, above all, why he had caused himself needless and unspeakable agony by crawling toward Uplands instead of lying where he had fallen. For some reason, it had been desperately important for him to reach the house.

She looked up eagerly when the doctor came in. He smiled reassuringly and told her that he had set Jarvis's leg and that in time he would be able to walk on it. He would not be crippled.

"Meanwhile," he said, "I'll call an ambulance and have him taken to the hospital."

"No," Penny said quickly. "Mr. Jarvis is my husband's oldest and most intimate friend. We'll look after him here."

"Then I'll see what I can do about getting hold of some good nurses."

Penny laughed. "My maid Nora, who used to be my nurse, will take care of him. She is highly qualified and conscientious and she would never forgive me if I didn't let her do this."

"Sure it won't be too much for you, having an invalid in the house?"

"Of course not. You don't think my husband would let him be taken away when we can look out for him ourselves?" She sounded indignant.

The doctor smiled. "Mr. Garth," he said, "is a very lucky man." He sobered. "I'd like to see this maid of yours and give her some instructions."

Penny rang and sent for Nora. In a moment she bustled into the room and the doctor gave her a keen glance and then smiled approval. He told her what would be needed and she nodded her head.

"I can manage without any trouble," she said. "I saw Penny—Mrs. Garth—through the measles and goodness knows what all, and nursed her brother with broken ribs and collar bones and once a broken arm. I know what to do."

"Then I'll get a night nurse to relieve you. I'll drop in later this afternoon to look over the patient."

"What happened, do you know?" Penny asked.

The doctor shook his head. "Mr. Jarvis wouldn't say. That reminds me, he wants to talk to you. I told him he'd better wait for a while but he said it was urgent. But just a few minutes, mind. No longer. I've given him a shot and he should be kept quiet until it can take effect."

Penny nodded. "I understand and I won't tire him."

"I'll see to that," Nora broke in. She sounded determined. "Ten minutes and no more, young lady."

The doctor laughed. "I see I am leaving my patient in competent hands."

When Penny tapped at the guest-room door Macy opened it for her. Jarvis lay in bed, his forehead bandaged, his face ghastly white, his leg in a cast and strapped to a pulley contraption.

"There you are, Penny," he called cheerfully, although his voice was very weak. "I won't need you, Macy."

The valet stood aside for Penny to enter the room and then went out, closing the door behind him.

Jarvis motioned for Penny to draw up a chair close to the bed. She sat down beside him.

"Geoff! I'm so terribly sorry. How did it happen?"

With a glance toward the door Jarvis raised his eyebrows. In surprise Penny got up and went noiselessly to the door.

Opened it. Macy, who had stooped to pick a thread off the carpet, got up and went on down the corridor to the back stairway without turning around. Penny looked after him thoughtfully, closed the door and returned to Jarvis.

He motioned for her to lean close to him. With his eyes on the door he whispered, "Steady, Penny! This is going to be a shock. I didn't intend to let you know but I'm out of the running now. I had to get here some way and warn you because from here on out it's up to you."

For a moment the girl thought that Jarvis was delirious with shock. His words sounded so absurd. But something in the anxious appeal in his eyes made her take him seriously.

"Someone—" he shaped the words carefully with his lips, no sound coming out, his eyes still sharp on the door— "someone mistook me for Don. I'd borrowed his car—mine's in the shop for a day—and it went out of control—brakes failed. No Garth car would be let out of his garage in that shape! Someone got at it and damaged the brake system."

Penny covered her mouth with her hand to choke back the cry that rose to her lips.

"I can't go into details now," Jarvis said, still in that almost soundless whisper, "I'll just give you the high lights. Don is in danger. Real danger. That's why I took that cottage so close to Uplands, why I've been hanging around here. I've been keeping an eye on him."

"Geoff!"

"It's not just my own idea," he went on. "Orders from the powers that be. They are building a new and revolutionary plane at the Works and there has been a leak somewhere. Too much information appears to be getting out and we can't find the missing link in the chain. But only Don knows the whole thing."

For a moment Penny's thoughts were in a whirl. She remembered Don explaining that the best security lay in the fact that only one man knew the whole picture. He had not told her that the man was himself!

"Without Don," Jarvis went on, speaking with effort, "there would be no plane. The country needs what he is doing now, Penny, and we've got to protect him."

He leaned back on his pillows, his face gray with pain and shock and anxiety.

"Geoff." Penny leaned forward, whispering too. "Then you are a government man."

"In a way." He was silent for a moment, exhausted, and then he began to talk again in his feverish whisper.

44

"Don's too valuable a man for us to take any chances with him. Someone has talked. There's a plan to get him on his way to or from the Works. No one could touch him once he gets there. And here—I think he is safe. But that trip between—think what it would mean to the country if anything happened to Don! He doesn't do the actual work but he's the brains, the spirit which keeps the men inspired and that great plant working to capacity. Penny—"

Again his head fell back on the pillows. He was so pale that she feared for a moment that he would faint.

"Later, Geoff," she told him soothingly. "You can tell me later when you are stronger."

He shook his head frantically. "There isn't—time. Penny—Penny, I want you to drive Don back and forth after this. You're so—popular with the men at the Works that no one would dare to touch you. He'll be safe if they know you're with him. You've—got to—watch out—for—"

"Don't talk any more, Geoff."

"Penny," he whispered hoarsely, "promise—"

Her hand closed firmly over his. "Geoff," she said, her voice clear and distinct so that the half-conscious man could understand her. "I promise. I won't fail."

He nodded, his eyes closed. His hand moved away from hers, clenched. "Penny, better keep an eye on him here at Uplands, too. I—think—it's all—right but—" He fought back waves of blackness. "Does he spend the evenings with you?"

The color flamed over her face, her neck, her forehead. "No, he works in his study."

"Then stay in there with him. Read. Play solitaire. Anything. Only stand by. Will you?"

"I don't know," she said slowly. "We have a house guest coming today. I'll have to spend part of my time with her or it will seem very odd."

"Can't you put her off? Tell your friend—"

"She isn't my friend. I've never seen her. She's a friend of Don's. Mrs. Thomas Scarlet."

"Kitty!" Geoffrey Jarvis stared at her unbelievingly. Penny stared back in equal surprise. The color flowed back into his face, the blurred eyes looked clear. He was like a man who had had a shot of adrenalin.

"Little Kitty Owens," he said softly. "Kitty Scarlet. I suppose you never knew her. You must have been away at school when she lived here and played havoc with all of us." He smiled.

His voice was stronger, his eyes alight. "Kitty!" his voice, Penny thought, sounded like Don's when he had spoken to the unknown woman over the telephone.

"Who is she, Geoff?"

"She married Tom Scarlet, an English diplomat, six years ago, but he died after two years of marriage. She has never come back to this country. And we never recuperated from Kitty. Though the one who raved and threatened was Dick Wentworth."

"Dick!" Penny exclaimed, stunned with surprise.

"Yes, Dick," he assured her dryly. "You see, Kitty had money, rafts of it. And Dick loves money—if he doesn't have to work for it. He had gone through everything he had and he was up to his ears in debt. He was so sure he'd get the Owens money in the long run that he was spending it before he persuaded Kitty to say yes. So after she married Tom Scarlet he had to cut expenses to the bone. He even had to give up his man, Macy."

Penny, dazed by her new knowledge of Dick Wentworth, said dully, "I didn't know Macy had been his man."

"Oh, yes. Don took him over when he was out of a job. Dick Wentworth left the poor guy high and dry without paying his salary and he practically begged Don to hire him. Since then, Wentworth has been trying his best to find a rich wife in Kitty's place."

"What—" Penny hesitated. "What is Kitty Scarlet like?"

"Didn't Don tell you? She's little and dainty and clinging, she has yellow hair and violet eyes, she's as gay as a Mardi Gras and as lighthearted as a soap bubble. You know the kind. Iridescent."

"No, I don't," Penny said crisply. "I don't have that devastating effect on men."

"Penny," Nora said protestingly from the doorway. "I mean—Mrs. Garth. The doctor said you were to be here only a few minutes. My patient needs rest and quiet."

Penny got to her feet, contritely. "I'm so sorry."

Jarvis clutched at her hand. "Promise?" he asked.

She nodded her head. "I promise."

Nora came forward, with a disapproving look at Penny, took Jarvis's wrist in her capable hand and looked at her watch. She was definitely in charge of the sickroom. With a last look at Geoff, lying exhausted on his pillows, Penny went quietly out.

Too restless to keep still, her thoughts in a turmoil, Penny went back to the garden and bent over a flower bed. Don was in danger, in terrible danger. Except for the sheer chance that had laid up Geoff's car and made him borrow one of Don's, it would have been Don who had been injured, perhaps killed.

She recalled the curious uneasiness that had driven her to go to the Works that morning and see for herself if Don were all right. It had been more than a premonition. And she had been right in thinking that Geoff was genuinely worried about his friend.

What a combination of keenness and boyishness Geoff was! Outwardly, he was an idle man of fortune, but suspicion had in this last hour attained to certainty in Penelope's mind. His indifferent manner was only a cover for earnest purpose. He was acting as a secret government agent.

And now he was helpless to carry on his task of protecting Don. He had put the responsibility in her hands. "Promise?" he had said urgently, and she had given him her solemn promise.

Before Garth's marriage, Jarvis had stayed at Uplands. At that time, he had moved to a charming cottage where he lived in luxurious comfort. He had made Penelope feel that he wanted to be most truly her friend. Did he suspect how things were between Don and her now? She had surprised his keen eyes on her face more than once. Whatever he knew, he probably blamed her. Well, she wouldn't skirt the fact that she was to blame. She had fancied herself madly in love with Dick Wentworth. Dick, the fortune hunter, who had tried to marry the fascinating Kitty Scarlet for her money!

Perhaps now, she thought, her face flaming, he believed she would divorce Don and marry him, bringing a large settlement on which he could live in comfort.

One thing she was sure of, that she was no longer in love with him. Perhaps her heart was burned out as far as love for any man was concerned.

With an impatient exclamation she forced her thoughts into other channels. What danger threatened the man she had married? She had promised to try to keep him with her. She! But how was she to do it? How was she to manage to drive him to the Works, spend the evenings with him in his study while he toiled over great batches of papers? Suppose she were to suggest it? She could imagine his expression, as warm as an able-bodied granite boulder. Or would he think —the color flamed to the roots of her hair.

What did it matter what he thought of her? Her feelings were not important. And something was wrong at Uplands. She had not been able to tell Geoff about seeing Fane load the revolver. He was too weak. As soon as he was stronger she would tell him. And there was more to it than that. Wherever she went, the butler seemed to emerge behind her as quietly as her own shadow and as close to her. And Macy had been listening outside the door of Geoff's room a few moments before.

Were there traitors in Don's own house? How was she to protect him from them? How was she to keep him with her under the circumstances of their marriage?

Anyhow, with Kitty Scarlet on the scene he would probably consider his wife a nuisance. She had destroyed the love he felt for her when they were married. She knew that. And Kitty, apparently, had won the hearts of all the men who had known her—Don as well as Geoff and Dick. Perhaps Don regretted now that he had married her before Kitty's return to America.

Penny's eyes were on the toe of the shoe with which she was viciously attacking an inoffensive dandelion which had had the effrontery to spring up in the velvet turf of the path. Why, she wondered at herself in surprise, did the thought of the unknown Kitty Scarlet fill her with such annoyance?

And behind her she heard a trill of silvery laughter.

She turned quickly and looked at the woman who stood facing her, a small golden-haired woman with enormous violet eyes. She wore a dress of lilac linen with a tiny hat perched on the yellow curls. She was lovely, Penny thought with a pang, aware of her own grubby hands, her gardening clothes, her gypsy skin warmed and darkened by the sun, the color that was so brilliant compared with the other woman's delicate tints.

"You must be Penelope Garth," the woman said with a bewitching smile.

"And you are Kitty Scarlet."

"You were so kind to let me come," the widow said vivaciously. "I was simply distracted. Washington is horribly crowded and I had no place to go while my house is being remodeled and redecorated. It's wonderful of you and Donald to have me."

"It is a great pleasure," Penny assured her, wishing she did not feel so young and gauche beside this poised woman of the world. But why, she wondered, if Mrs. Scarlet was so extremely wealthy, did she claim to have no place to go? And if that was not true, why had she chosen to come to Uplands?

Aloud she said, "There's another friend of yours here who is looking forward to seeing you."

It seemed to Penny that the young widow was rigid, curiously still for a moment, her lovely face a careful blank. Then she asked casually, "And who is that?"

"Geoffrey Jarvis."

Kitty Scarlet smiled radiantly. "Dear Geoff! How delightful. Where is he? I can't wait."

"I'm afraid you can't see him today," Penny said and explained briefly about his accident.

"Geoff!" The violet eyes widened in amazement. "But he is a fanatic about keeping his cars in perfect condition; he's always checking them and tinkering with them. How on earth—"

"It wasn't his car. He borrowed one of Don's," Penny began and then wished she had not said anything. Geoff had not told her to keep still about his using Don's car but something in Kitty's face bothered her, a curious speculative look that passed over it and then was gone.

Penny led her guest back to the house, where she met the widow's mother. Mrs. Owens, tall and stately and white-haired, did not resemble her diminutive and vivacious daughter. She was a handsome, almost a regal-looking woman, Penny thought, with an innate graciousness of manner which won the girl's heart at once. The only likeness to her daughter was in the same immense violet eyes.

When Penny had escorted the two women to their rooms, she tapped at Geoff's door. Nora opened it and slipped quietly into the hall.

"He's asleep," she said in a low tone. "That medicine the doctor gave him finally got in its work." She gave Penny a reproachful look. "But you shouldn't have kept him talking so long."

"I'll have a nurse here tonight to relieve you," Penny promised.

"That won't be necessary. Macy is going to lend a hand. He didn't want to," the nurse said grimly, "but I told him what I expected and he agreed."

"You don't seem to like him any better than I do," Penny said.

"Wouldn't trust him as far as I could throw him," Nora

admitted. "Face like a rodent. Not that he can help his face," she conceded, "but anyone can help his expression."

Nora studied Penny for a moment, head on one side. "So your guests have come. I had the door open when they came past. That young one is a raving beauty."

Penny's heart dropped like a rock. "Yes, she's lovely—to look at."

"I've told you before," Nora scolded her, "not to be green-eyed. Jealousy is not a nice quality."

Penny giggled in spite of herself. "Nora, will you ever remember I'm grown up—a married woman?"

The nurse smiled reluctantly. "I guess not," she said. "You run along now and don't worry about Mr. Jarvis."

Penny went on to her own rooms, showered and changed to a tan cotton afternoon dress. She brushed her dark hair until it sparkled. Then she studied herself in the mirror with dissatisfaction, the skin warmed by the sun, the bright color in cheek and lip, and thought of the pastel shades of the charming Mrs. Scarlet.

She went downstairs to order tea served on the terrace.

Fane said, "There's an—individual down at the garage, madam, looking for you. He's been hanging around for an hour and refused to leave. He said you had given instructions that he could come here to visit his dog."

"So I did," Penny said. "I'll see him now."

The butler opened his lips almost as though he were about to protest and then wheeled and went quietly out of the room. Beside the garage Penny found the young draftsman on his knees, stroking the dog, which was frantic with delight. He straightened up as soon as he saw her.

"Vag is getting along beautifully," Penny assured him in her warm, friendly voice. "The veterinary says he'll have the wound healed before long and then you can take him home."

For a moment the troubled eyes met hers and looked away again. "I wish I knew how to thank you, Mrs. Garth," he said. "Vag's all I have."

"I love dogs, too," Penny told him. "And this one is a honey." She stooped down, forgetful of the fresh dress, and patted the dog's head. It looked up at her with wistful eyes.

"Well . . ." The draftsman stood twisting his cap in his hands as though ill at ease. His eyes traveled over the great sweep of velvet lawn, over the big garage. At the moment there were only two cars in it. Don had driven himself to work in the third. The fourth, the one in which Geoff had

50

so nearly been killed, had been taken by a wrecker to the village garage for repairs.

"Your chauffeur"—again the expressive hands twisted the cap as though wringing it dry of water—"says there was an accident to one of your cars."

"Yes, a friend of my husband's was driving it and he was nearly killed."

"I told your chauffeur, these are queer times; it would be wise to check a car thoroughly before it is taken out. And he said he'd do it from now on. It's a—wise precaution."

Without intending to do so, Penny heard herself saying, "From now on I'm going to drive my husband to work. Men are more—careless—than women." She turned away with a smiling nod and went back to the house and her guests.

Petro looked after her, watching the gallant lift of her chin, the indefinable thing that means character.

"She's a very nice lady," he said to the chauffeur. "I'm glad she wasn't in the car that was wrecked."

"No car here will get wrecked again," the chauffeur said grimly. "Someone had been at those brakes. I know it. I keep the cars in perfect condition. After this, I'll check everything before she so much as starts out. Mrs. Garth is the apple of the Chief's eye. Anyone can tell how he feels about her, all right. It's heart-warming to see a marriage like that. One that nothing can spoil."

"One that nothing can spoil," Petro repeated. He waved his hand and started off along the driveway, his head bowed in thought.

"Hey," the chauffeur called, "that's not the way to the road."

But the young draftsman was already out of sight.

VIII

That evening Penny took more trouble than ever in her life while she dressed for dinner. For some reason, which she did not want to analyze to herself, it was imperative that she should look her best. Not even on her wedding day had she spent so much time brushing her hair and arranging it.

Her wedding day! She put down her brush and stared unseeingly at the girl in the mirror as she had done on that day

51

weeks before. How frightened she had been, and how heart-sick. With the loss of Dick Wentworth it had seemed to her that all the years ahead would be empty. And Dick himself had entered the room, killing her love for him by revealing the man he really was. If only she could have explained to Don what had happened to her during that interview. Would it change him? Would he lose his wooden politeness, his granite reserve? Would it—matter to him?

There had been that magic moment in his study when he had seen the bruises he had made on her arms, when he had kissed them. Her pulses leaped even now as she remembered it. And then Fane had come in with that letter from Dick Wentworth, the letter she had never answered, and the warmth had left his eyes; he was the icy Don he had been ever since.

Except, she thought with a little pang, when he had spoken to Kitty Scarlet on the telephone. No one could have called him icy then.

She opened her wardrobe and reached for a white dinner dress with long, simple lines. For a moment she studied it and then, impulsively, put it back and took out a filmy red dress, low-cut, with a flaring skirt that swept the ground and swirled around her like a cloud blazing at sunset. It made her dark skin and hair and eyes dramatic. She smiled at herself. Let Kitty match that, she told herself, the dimples showing deep in her cheeks while she laughed mischievously.

For a moment she considered going down to Don's study and asking for the jewel case. Then she changed her mind. She could not hope to rival Kitty Scarlet at sophistication. But why, she wondered, did it seem important to regard Kitty as a rival?

Kitty! Penny's brief moment of triumph was over. How could she compete with anyone as fascinating as Kitty? Nora had called her a raving beauty. Even in his pain and shock, Geoffrey Jarvis had brightened at the thought of her arrival. Dick Wentworth, according to Geoff, had made a terrible and dramatic scene when she had married Tom Scarlet, the English diplomat. And Don—what had Don felt?

He was alone in the drawing room when she entered, tall and stern and better-looking than she had remembered. As usual his dinner clothes fitted beautifully. He was looking out at the glory of the sunset but he seemed unaware of it. His thoughts were troubled. At her step he turned tensely and then he relaxed. For a moment there was a light in his eyes as he looked at her.

"Penelope! You are beauti—" He checked himself. "That dress is a great success," he added huskily.

"Thank you, Don." She turned slowly for his approval, skirts swirling like leaping flames, and looked up at him from under long lashes. "I'm glad you approve of me."

He took a step forward, smiling down at her, and there was no more granite in his expression.

Something in his look made her oddly breathless. "Don," she said quickly, "have you heard about Geoff?"

"About Geoff?" he said in surprise. "No, what has he been up to?"

She told him about the accident and that Jarvis was now installed in a guest room at Uplands with Nora and Macy looking after him.

"I thought you would want him here," she concluded, "instead of in a hospital."

"Of course," he agreed. "You were quite right. But I don't understand how it could have happened. If you'd see the way he takes care of his car—watching every little thing."

"It wasn't his car—it was your two-seater."

Don gave a low exclamation, whistled. "I had intended to drive that myself this morning. I almost always do, but I took the bigger car because I planned to pick up a couple of men."

He reached for her quickly, holding her by the arms. "Hey, you aren't going to faint, are you? You're as white as a ghost. Better sit down."

"I'm all right." She clutched at his coat. "Don," she whispered through dry lips, "it might have been you. It was supposed to be you. The chauffeur says the brakes had been tampered with. It wasn't—just an accident."

Don's eyes continued to meet hers but Penny felt that he no longer saw her. He was looking at some inner picture of his own. His mouth tightened until it seemed sterner, harder than she had ever seen it.

"So that's it," he said at last. "So that's it."

"What is?" called a gay voice and Kitty Scarlet came into the room with her mother.

The young widow wore a strapless dress of ice blue, a diamond necklace glittered on her beautiful neck, and long diamond earrings swung at her ears. Her yellow hair was swept high on her head in tiny curls. The fragrance of a light, pungent perfume swept into the room with her. She was,

53

Penny thought, a raving beauty as Nora had said. Lovely and gay. An iridescent soap bubble.

Behind her stood her mother in a gray crepe dinner dress with a train, pearls hanging in a long matched string almost to her waist. Her white hair was becomingly arranged and she moved with stately grace.

"Mrs. Owens!" Don crossed the room eagerly and raised her hand to his lips. "Welcome to Uplands! My wife and I are so happy to have you with us." He turned to Kitty and took both hands in his. "Kitty! You are more ravishing than ever. How do you manage to go on looking as though you weren't a day over eighteen? You make me feel a stodgy middle age."

"Don't be ridiculous, Don," the widow said with a gay laugh. "You are still the best-looking man I know." She tipped her head a little to one side. "Marriage agrees with you," she added. "And I haven't had a chance yet to congratulate you on winning so charming a bride."

To Penny's ears the words had a slightly patronizing sound.

"Thank you, Kitty," Don said; the gaiety had left his voice, it was grave and remote once more.

It seemed to Penny that the conversation during dinner was a duet between Kitty and Don, a series of "Do you remember" stories about parties and old jokes and mutual friends, all of which was new to Penny and made her feel left out.

Kitty's mother, who was keenly observant, noticed it and, after an odd look at her daughter, took pains to draw Penny out about her garden; her brother, who had been called into the service and was going through basic training; her mother, who was recuperating, but so slowly, from a dangerous operation.

Don looked up once from his absorbing banter with Kitty to say, "Mrs. Owens, you must get Penelope to tell you what she is doing in the village."

That was the only break in the eager talk between Kitty and Don and the more forced conversation between Penny and the tactful Mrs. Owens. Penny tried to keep her mind on her guests but she found herself being watchful, trying to account for the curious incident that had occurred just before they entered the dining room.

They had been talking in the drawing room when Fane appeared in the doorway to announce dinner and caught his first sight of Kitty. Because she had wandered around to the garden on her arrival and Penny had taken her to her room, the butler had not seen her until this moment. He looked at her and Penny would have sworn there was recognition in his eyes, recognition and a kind of shock.

For a moment he had stood motionless, swallowing. Then he said with grave impersonality, "Dinner is served," and Don offered his arm to Mrs. Owens. So far as Penny was aware, none of the others had noticed Fane's manner.

All during dinner she kept taking surreptitious glances at him, but the butler managed things with his usual smoothness, directing the waitress in an almost imperceptible undertone. He had not once looked at Mrs. Kitty Scarlet.

ii

The next morning was one of those perfect June days. Penny woke early, nagged by an unsolved puzzle. How was she to keep her promise to Geoffrey Jarvis?

She got up at six, dressed in a Dutch-blue tailored skirt and matching sweater, and went out in the garden to fortify herself by its beauty for the coming interview. The sky was a deep cloudless blue, the roses a fragrant glory, not only those in the beds but the climbers along the stone fence and over the side of the garage. Birds were singing their morning carol of gladness to the sun and dew still glistened on the grass.

Penny put her hand to her throat which ached with so much beauty. The sound of a footstep made her turn and she found Don beside her.

"Good morning, Penelope," he said with a touch of tenderness she had never heard before in his voice. "Your long eyelashes are sparkling with tears just as the grass is with the dew. Is all this beauty too much for you?"

"It's lovely, isn't it, Don?"

"Very lovely," he said, his eyes still on her face and a little smile on his lips.

She felt herself blushing. Don's smile deepened. He laughed. "Can't I tell my wife she is lovely without causing so much confusion?"

Penny looked away and Don said, to relieve her embarrassment, "Hawkins tells me this is all your work."

She nodded. "I wanted to make Uplands warm and beautiful for you."

"You have," he said gruffly.

She took a long breath. Penny, she told herself firmly, you've got to do it and this is your only chance. Remember—you promised.

She gripped her hands tight behind her. "Don," she plunged, "will you let me drive you back and forth to the Works in the convertible?" Her face was flushed, her eyes shy and earnest as they met his. "I really haven't enough to do, even with the garden and planning the village projects. They take so long to get started. And there isn't enough to keep me—"

"To keep you from thinking of Wentworth?" he interrupted and his words were like a blow.

Penelope opened her lips in indignant denial, remembered her promise to Geoff and closed them. She had sworn that she would do her best to protect Donald Garth. She must not quarrel with him. Even though the wall still stood between them, so high there was no glimpsing the top, there had, for a moment, been a crack in it through which they could see one another.

"Geoff told me," she said quietly, "about the danger you are in."

"Geoff," he raged. "I would not have believed it of him."

"Don," she wailed, her hand catching at his sleeve. "Don't go away like that, all granity, and cold steel, and ice. I'm not a child. Geoff told me because he can't keep an eye on you himself. Let me drive you, Don! They won't hurt me. Geoff was sure of that."

"Do you think for a single moment that I would deliberately let you run into danger?"

"But there is no danger. Let me do my part, Don. Please. Please. You are doing yours so—so magnificently." She brushed tears from her eyes. "I'm proud of you. Let me be —a little—proud of myself, too. There's no danger to me."

He looked down at her intently, his brows drawn together in a frown. He shook his head.

"Don," she persisted, "you can't just think of your pride. The Works and what you are doing there—what your family has done for generations—what you still have to accomplish—the country needs all that. You have no right to make this decision without thinking of all those things."

There was a strange look in his face, one she had never seen before. At length he nodded, unsmiling. "All right," he said curtly. "We'd better have breakfast together after this. And after breakfast bring the car to the door."

iii

On her return to Uplands after leaving Don at the Works, Penny was surprised to find Nora in her dressing room, mending a rip in one of her dresses.

"Is Mr. Jarvis asleep?" she asked.

Nora shrugged. "Not when I saw him last," she said dryly. "That Mrs. Scarlet came breezing in there and took charge." Nora sniffed. "She said she would look after Mr. Jarvis and call me if she needed me."

"How is he today?"

"He is in a lot of pain but he doesn't mention it. Just jokes and is as nice and pleasant as can be. He won't ask for a thing for fear it's too much trouble. That's a nice man, Penny —Mrs. Garth."

"Yes, he is," Penny agreed.

Nora kept her eyes on her mending. "I'm glad Mr. Garth has a friend like that."

Penny, changing to gardening clothes, made no answer, though, in the mirror, she could see Nora studying her covertly.

After a little pause Nora said, "That man Wentworth—"

"I never want to hear his name again," Penny said crisply. "I made an awful mistake and I—" she choked—"I guess I'll pay for it all my life."

"Then you don't love him any more?" The woman who had been Penny's nurse beamed. "The Lord be praised!"

Penny gave her a little hug. "I don't know what I'd do without you, Nora."

"You'd go right on being the sunny-hearted, brave girl you are now," the older woman said stoutly. "I guess I know all there is to know about you, Penny—Mrs. Garth; those level eyes and tender lips and the courage you've got to take it even when it's hard and you don't see a way out. You're like your mother in that way. Look how she faced that operation: not a word of complaint, not a sign of fear. When I was there at the hospital, the doctor told me he sometimes sent other patients in to see her just because she had a way of lifting their hearts for 'em. It's that character that is helping her to get well as much as it is the operation."

Penny smiled through her tears. "Marmee is pretty wonderful."

"And you'll be just like her. I can tell you I had an awful sick feeling on your wedding day when I misjudged you."

Penny picked up her gardening gloves. "Are you sure you

57

are getting enough rest? Isn't looking after Mr. Jarvis going to be too much for you?"

"Nonsense. As I told you, he's a model patient. Anyhow, your husband has instructed his man, Macy, to give me any help I need. I must say," she added grudgingly, "I can't stand the man but he is efficient."

"I know how you feel," Penny agreed. "For some reason I can't trust him."

She ran down the stairs and out to the garden, where Mrs. Owens was strolling around, admiring the roses. "Isn't Kitty with you?" she asked in surprise.

"She has gone to see our patient," Penny said gaily. "I know poor Geoff will be delighted."

Mrs. Owens nodded calmly as though this were the most natural thing in the world. "Yes," she agreed, "Kitty is excellent in a sickroom."

Penny flashed a surprised look at her and went on clipping roses. Anything less suited for a sickroom than Mrs. Thomas Scarlet she had never encountered. The widow belonged in a ballroom, flirting vivaciously with every man in sight. Penny snipped hard at the stem of a rose.

"Kitty," the older woman went on, "is not the butterfly she appears to be. Far from it."

"Then why," Penny began impulsively and did not know how to finish her question.

Mrs. Owens was troubled. She bit her lips. "I don't know," she said, shaking her head. She added gravely, "I don't know. She has changed in some way."

But it was not merely in a ballroom that Kitty could flirt, as Penny realized later that day when she drove Don home from the Works. As the car turned in at the gates, there was a gay call and Penelope stepped on the brake with startling suddenness. Kitty had darted out from behind some shrubs into the very path of the car. She wore a violet organdy dress and a big shade hat that was extravagantly becoming. She waved a rosebud merrily in one hand.

Don opened the door and she slid into the broad seat beside him. She turned to put the rosebud in his buttonhole. Then she looked up as though only then aware of Penelope's presence.

"Oh hello, Mrs. Garth. Wonderful weather, isn't it? We ought to do something to celebrate it."

"That is definitely an idea," Don said promptly. "Penelope, why don't we arrange a garden party in honor of our adorable guest?"

Kitty clapped her hands. "Oh, Don, how wonderful! I've got a marvelous dress just crying for a garden party. And an orchestra out of doors and dancing on the terrace. You know how I love dancing out of doors."

She laid one tiny pink-tipped white hand on Don's and Penny contrasted it with her own sun-browned hand on the wheel. She always felt like a splashy chromo beside an exquisite water color when the widow was around, and the fact made her furiously angry with herself. Green-eyed, she told herself in annoyance. Why, she asked herself, should she care? It was ridiculous.

"Of course," she said aloud in belated answer to Don's suggestion. "I'll plan a garden party for Midsummer's eve. The weather should be perfect and there will be a full moon. Give me your guest list in the morning, Don." She added politely, "And yours, Mrs. Scarlet. If you have any friends near Uplands, I should be delighted to entertain them, too."

At least, she thought, she was reminding Mrs. Scarlet that she was the hostess at Uplands. She was aware of a curious, half-laughing glance from Don, which vanished so quickly that she was not sure she had not imagined it.

She stopped in front of the house and Kitty got out and ran up the steps to the front door. Don followed more slowly. He took the rosebud out of his buttonhole, hesitated, and then, pulling out his billfold, carefully tucked it inside. Then he followed the widow into the house.

IX

Penny stood on the small balcony outside her sitting room, taking a bird's-eye view of the arrangements for the garden party. The day had been made to order, she thought. She looked down at the sun-drenched velvety lawn with its magnificent rose garden, the great elm trees throwing a stately shade, at the bright canopies, the gay-colored chairs and tables, the elaborately arranged buffet table at the far end of the lawn and, on the terrace, the orchestra members in their white coats, already tuning up to provide Strauss waltzes and later music for dancing.

"What a heavenly day," she thought. "I hope, for Don's sake, the first big party which I have planned will be a success." Her bright face clouded when she remembered that

59

the party was being given, at his suggestion, in honor of Kitty Scarlet, but she refused to have the glorious day shaded. She herself was to meet for the first time many of their neighbors and some of Don's old friends and she wanted, with all her heart, to make him proud of his wife.

Looking down at the sun-splashed garden she quoted softly:

> "And what is so rare as a day in June?
>   Then, if ever, come perfect days;
> Then Heaven tries the earth if it be in tune,
>   And over it softly her warm ear lays:
> Whether we look, or whether we listen,
> We hear life murmur, or see it glisten . . ."

She left her room and knocked at Geoffrey Jarvis's door. In a moment Macy opened it wide and pushed out a wheelchair in which Geoff sat, dressed in a white linen suit, smiling at her.

"All set for the big day," he cried cheerfully, "and I'm looking forward to it, Lucky Penny."

"Grand; it would be a failure without you, Geoff. I'm a little nervous about my first big affair and I'm counting on a wonderful party man like you to help keep things going."

"Well," he drawled, laughing, "you'll have to rely solely on my charm. It's a cinch I can't dance with the wallflowers." He looked down at the leg in its cast.

"All I'm afraid of," she retorted, "is that you will prove to be such a big attraction that I won't be able to persuade any of the women to dance. And guess who's coming?" she asked gaily. "Terry himself! His first leave."

She waited until Macy had pushed the wheelchair into the elevator and left Geoff with a wave of the hand which he answered with a mock salute as the elevator door closed. Don joined her at the foot of the stairs where he was waiting with Kitty and her mother. The latter turned the violet eyes that were so disturbingly like her daughter's from Penny's face to Don's, with a searching look. She wore a thoughtful expression as she went out onto the lawn at Don's side while Kitty followed with Penny, chatting vivaciously.

Penelope received the guests in company with Mrs. Scarlet in the shadow of a mammoth oak. A mass of rhododendrons with their dark leaves and brilliant blossoms made an effective background for the two slender figures: the dark-haired girl in white, the widow in pale green, which reduced the other women present to speechlessness.

Even in the midst of her rather arduous duties, Penelope appreciated the fact that it was an education in social graces to stand beside Mrs. Scarlet and hear her greet the guests. She had a special thought and word for each one and, much as Penny distrusted and disliked the woman, she had to acknowledge that she shaded her tone to a nicety to carry conviction.

Penny was busy greeting people whom she already knew and those who were as yet strangers to her, each of whom had a warm word of welcome for the girl who had become Donald Garth's wife.

If this were a real marriage, she thought, how heartwarming it would be to have all these pleasant things said to me. But I know they don't apply to me. I'm not Don's wife, just a guest in his house. Like—like Kitty.

Penelope was being held in conversation. A hot, chubby hand clutched hers while its owner, a Rubensesque dowager, descanted upon her physical disabilities. Above the rather deep voice of the dowager rang Kitty's high sweet tones.

"Dick Wentworth! Hello, stranger! How wonderful to see you after all this time."

Penelope never knew the conclusion of the tragic history of the stout guest's fallen arches. She turned away from the dowager with a suddenness which caused that lady to swallow a word in her surprise. The girl felt as though every drop of blood in her body rushed to her head in a torrential tide. Dick Wentworth here! Who had invited him? His name had not appeared on her own guest list or on Don's. Kitty had sent personal messages to some of the people on her own list. Could she be responsible for his presence?

Penny glanced from under her long lashes at Don. There was a white line about his lips, a stony look in his eyes as they sought hers. Surely, surely he did not believe that she was capable of inviting Dick Wentworth to Uplands, to Don's own house! She had never even answered his letter.

Dick was beside her now, smiling down at her with an expression that, so few weeks ago, would have made her heart shake. It did nothing to her heart now. She was cold with anger at him for coming here, whether or not Kitty had sent him an invitation. He had no right in this house. No one knew that better than he. The smile that had once so charmed her now seemed self-consciously attractive; the eyes

61

that had thrilled her seemed watchful, wary, coldly calculating. But he was, she remembered, her guest.

She held out her hand and steadied the quiver of her voice. "This is a surprise, Dick! She could not bring herself to say, "How nice of you to come," or any of the usual words of greeting.

Out of the corner of her eye she saw Don turn on his heel and move away to talk to a group of guests who were admiring the roses.

Dick's hand held hers so tightly that he almost crushed it. "Penny!" he said in a low voice. "Penny, my darling. Did you think I wouldn't come?" In spite of himself an exultant note crept into his voice. "I knew you would send for me, sooner or later."

She jerked her hand away and he was forced to move on, to bow to Mrs. Owens, whose manner was stately, even chilly, when she greeted him. After exchanging as few words as the occasion permitted, Dick went on hastily. Penny noticed that he carefully avoided the group of laughing people clustered around Geoffrey Jarvis's wheelchair.

She stole a quick look at Kitty Scarlet, who was pressing a filmy handkerchief to her lips. The girl had a horrible suspicion that the widow was stifling a laugh. Her face crimsoned as her guest turned to her with cool, amused eyes.

"So Dick has been making love to you, too, has he? Love with him isn't a passion, it's a habit. Don't take him too seriously, my dear." The velvet smoothness of her tone made her hostess feel very young and raw and crude.

"I wouldn't take him any way," she snapped, and then was ashamed of herself for losing her temper.

As the afternoon waned Penelope passed from group to group. As she increased the distance between herself and the widow she slipped naturally into the gracious charm of manner characteristic of her and as remote from Mrs. Scarlet's effusive one as the stars are from an arc light. For the first time since she had married Donald Garth she had a sense of reality, of having come into her own. She knew now that she no longer felt a vestige of love for Dick Wentworth. She was free forever from that emotional strain. From now on she could live her life coolly and happily.

Her heart felt as though it had achieved wings. Her beautiful face was radiant as she approached her brother Terry, very proud of his uniform, who was in devoted attendance upon a pretty, long-legged girl who looked like nothing so much as an elongated Alice in Wonderland.

Penny stood on tiptoe to inspect her brother and said in an awed whisper, "Is it—can it be—is that the beginning of a mustache?"

Terry turned scarlet. Then he said with mock humility, "A small thing but mine own." He hugged her. "You look like the Queen of Sheba. Dolly and I caught the blaze of your earrings through the shrubs. What diamonds!"

"The Garth jewels," breathed Dolly.

"Do you like them?" Penny said to the girl, whose eyes were great lamps of admiration as she fixed them on the long dangling diamond and pearl pendants in the ears of her hostess.

"Like them! Oh, Mrs. Garth—" The words ended in a wail of longing. "They are the most thrilling things I ever saw. I'm crazy about earrings. I guess every girl is since Queen Elizabeth has made them so fashionable. But Mother won't even let me look at them yet."

"Well, don't cry about it. You'll grow up sometime," adjured Terry with lordly brutality. "Penny, to get back to more important matters, when do we eat?"

She laughed. "Don't you ever think of anything else?"

"Not often."

Penny tucked one arm under his and one under Dolly's and led them across the lawn to the buffet table where several waiters were busy. She looked around for Fane, who should have been supervising, but he was not in sight. Odd, she thought. It was unlike the butler to be slack in his duties.

The long table with its snowy cloth and massed flowers was laden with chafing dishes of creamed oysters, platters of cold smoked turkey, tiny caviar sandwiches, exotic fishes, hams, little sausages.

"Just like the army," commented Terry with a laugh. "Let's start, Dolly, before the crowd descends on us and cleans the place out like a plague of locusts."

"Madam," said a quiet voice, and Penny turned to find Fane at her side. "The—individual who owns the mongrel has come to get it."

Penny nodded. "I'll see him, Fane. Anyhow," she laughed, "I want to say good-by to Vag."

She took a quick look across the lawn before she left. Her guests seemed to be enjoying themselves. A little group was occupied with the croquet game, others were having their fortunes told in a bright-colored tent, still others were beginning to gather at the buffet table or were wandering in twos and threes through the rose garden.

She did not see Don or Kitty or Dick Wentworth. Mrs. Owens was moving from group to group with social ease. Geoff in his wheelchair was holding court to a group of laughing friends. The party was a success, she told herself. A smashing success. In being a hostess, at least, she had not failed Don.

With the sound of a Strauss waltz "Artist's Life," lilting in her ears, she went through the shrubbery toward the garage. Stopped. Checked herself. Beside her the shrubs rustled. People were whispering. She held her breath. There was something furtive, disturbing in the sound. Then a man's voice said, "Risky, very risky." There was a muttered sound and a few words, "—no other way."

A twig caught on Penny's skirt and the material rustled softly. The voices broke off. There was a movement in the shrubbery and Macy darted out, his head ducked as though he hoped not to be recognized, and passed around the side of the lawn, running back toward the house, keeping on the outskirts of the crowd.

Macy! Penny frowned. What was he doing here? She had never trusted him. What was he talking about? What risk? What was being plotted? She thought of Geoff's warning. Somehow she must get to him, tell him what she had overheard. She remembered then that as yet she had told no one about Fane loading the revolver, about his strange look of surprise when he had first seen Kitty. The butler and Kitty? She must be crazy. There could not possibly be any connection between the servant and the wealthy widow.

And if there were, she thought slowly, she could hardly tell Don. He might think she was jealous. Geoff! She would tell Geoff.

She heard a dog barking and went on toward the garage. Vag was racing wildly around, as far as the rope tied to his collar would let him go, barking excitedly. There was no sign of Vag's young master.

"Vag!" she called. "Vag!"

The dog leaped toward her, wagging its tail. Forgetful of the fragile dress, she dropped down beside him, scratching his head, patting him.

"Why are you making so much noise?" she chided him. "And where is your master?"

There was a stealthy sound that brought her heart into her throat and then Petro, white-faced, slipped into sight and unfastened the dog from its rope.

He was so ghastly white that Penny said in her warm, sympathetic voice, "You look ill. Let me call someone. Perhaps some coffee—"

"No," he said harshly, as though terror-stricken. "No, don't call anyone, madam. Please, don't call anyone. I'm all right." His voice was so low she could barely hear it.

"If you are sure—"

"Quite sure. I'm grateful for what you've done for Vag, Mrs. Garth. I can't put it into words. But I'll prove it in actions." His burning eyes met hers earnestly. There was a step behind her and without a word, clutching the dog's collar, the man darted out of sight.

Well, thought Penny, bewildered. Well! Who on earth can have frightened the poor man so much? He was hiding from someone when I came. Now he runs away. She shook her head, puzzled, and got slowly to her feet. As she turned around, Fane was moving away from her, going back toward the house.

X

Penelope pushed open the gate of the rose garden and paused, gazing thoughtfully after the butler as he went back to his neglected duties. Who and what was Fane? Was he the one who frightened the young draftsman who owned Vag? For no one could mistake that white, stricken face, the fact that he had taken flight when he heard someone approach. Anyhow, why did Fane persist in following her around? Fane and Macy—something was very wrong with those two men. Surely they ought not to be allowed to stay at Uplands at a time when Don was in danger.

Penny started through the gate absent-mindedly, head down, lips tense. A stifled exclamation brought her eyes up to the handsome, triumphant face of Dick Wentworth. She recoiled a step.

"Well, darling, here I am!" he said, holding out his hands. "I thought you would never send for me. You can't imagine my relief when that invitation came. I knew what it meant."

She stood very straight, her eyes meeting his steadily. "I did not send for you, Dick. I meant it when I told you that I would not see you again—ever. That my feeling for you was over. You had no right to send me that letter. It must never happen again."

His hand caught hers so firmly that she could not withdraw it.

"Tell me the truth, Penny. Why did you ask me to this party if you really mean that you are done with me?" He smiled, sure of his influence over her.

"I did not ask you, Dick. I did not send you the invitation. I never dreamed that you were coming. Perhaps your friend Kitty—"

His mouth tightened. "I've been talking to Kitty and that iceberg of a mother of hers. Mrs. Owens always hated me. Called me a fortune hunter, among other things." He laughed angrily. "Kitty says she warned you about me. You won't pay any attention to her, will you, Penny? Lovely Penny! You know her game, don't you? You know why she's come back from Europe. She wants Don. Don't believe what she says about me—about anything. Don't believe her mother, either."

"Mrs. Scarlet is my guest, Dick," Penny said, her heart racing with fury. "So is Mrs. Owens. And I am Donald Garth's wife. Please remember that in the future. And never —never dare come to Uplands again."

"Pen!" Dick's face was strained, incredulous. "Pen, you can't mean that. I love you. You love—"

"Don't finish that sentence, Dick!" There was a suggestion of steel in the musical voice.

"Deny that you love me, if you can," he challenged. He drew her closer to him. "Deny it if you can," he repeated nervously. "But you can't deny that I love you, Penny. I adore you. Do you think Garth would ever have got you if I had not been up to my ears in debt? Not a chance."

Penelope was furiously angry.

"Don't speak as though I were a piece of merchandise to be knocked down to the highest bidder," she protested hotly. Then a thought sent the blood in a crimson wave to her hair.

Wentworth stared at her pitilessly. He shrugged his shoulders.

"I see from your expression that it is unnecessary for me to remind you of the humor of that remark in the light of what really happened." He seized her and drew her close until her head was pressed against his shoulder.

"Dick! Dick! Don't dare—" The girl exerted all her strength to free herself.

Behind them came a silvery laugh. "Dick, Dick," Kitty repeated mockingly, "up to your old tricks, I see."

With a muttered exclamation Wentworth released Penelope. Then he turned with an easy laugh and offered his arm to Mrs. Scarlet. "Surely," he said sarcastically, "you have taken as much of Garth's time and attention as you should. Even as the guest of honor you must remember that he is supposed to be a happy bridegroom." He laughed again, bringing the color flaming into the face of the man beside Kitty.

For a moment Penny thought that Donald Garth would lunge at the impudent, insulting face of the man who was reminding him, so insolently, that she had not married him for love. She moved quickly, laid her hand on her husband's arm.

"Don," she said lightly, "I'm so glad you came. I want to start the dancing and I thought—people will expect us to lead the way. Shall we—?"

Slowly the clenched hand relaxed. He offered her his arm. She laid her fingers lightly on it. Below the sleeve she could feel the bunched muscle. They walked without a word through the garden to the dancing pavilion where, at a signal from Penny, the orchestra broke into the strains of "People Will Say We're in Love."

Don took her in his arms and they swept across the dance floor which had been laid for the occasion. Slowly the other guests, attracted by the dance rhythms of the orchestra and the swirling, dipping couple on the platform lighted by Japanese lanterns, gathered and began to dance.

Dancing has never been like this before, Penny realized, as she floated rather than moved across the platform in perfect time to the music. Why—this is the first time I have ever danced with Don!

Slowly the hard muscle in his arm relaxed, he held her closer, his dark head bent over hers, side-stepping, turning, gliding.

"Our first dance," she said with a gay little laugh. She looked up at his face and the words stopped on her lips. "Don," she whispered, shocked. "What's wrong?"

"Why did you invite Dick Wentworth to my—to our— house?"

"I didn't invite him. I never dreamed that he was coming. It was as much of a surprise to me as it was to you."

He laughed.

"Don, don't you believe me?"

"How can I? That letter he wrote—I couldn't help seeing it. He said to send him a word."

"But I didn't. I didn't!"

"And he just crashed the party without being sure what your feelings were?"

"I didn't ask him," Penny said coldly.

"But someone—"

"Ask your friend Mrs. Scarlet."

Don missed a step, went on. His face lighted, years seemed to drop off. "Penelope! Do you really mean to tell me—"

"I shouldn't have to tell you," she said stormily. "If you think I'd do a contemptible thing like that, that I have so little loyalty—"

"Sorry," he said. "I supposed—"

"Don," she said, her voice broken by a sob, "even if you can't love me any more, you can trust me!"

Tears were streaming down her cheeks. To escape the curious eyes of her guests, she broke away from him and ran off the platform, down into the almost deserted rose garden.

"Whoa," a gay voice called as she almost careened into Geoff's wheelchair.

She blinked the tears out of her eyes, and curled up on the grass at his feet.

"What's gone wrong?" he asked, the banter fading as he saw the tears.

Curiously enough, Penny found that her anger was directed not at Don for his lack of trust but, without any excuse at all, at Kitty Scarlet.

"Oh, Geoff," she wailed, "she's a cat. A cat!"

His hand, thinner since the accident, touched her dark hair lightly. "Who's a cat, Lucky Penny?"

The girl was too furiously angry and humiliated to be diverted by his flippancy. It was so unjust that she should be blamed for that invitation to Dick Wentworth when it was obviously Kitty who, for some unknown reason of her own, had sent it.

Could it be sheer chance that had brought Kitty and Don into the garden just as Dick was making love to her? Or had Kitty planned it deliberately? Dick said she wanted Don. That she had come back from England to get him. What better way to get him than to have him witness a scene like that, particularly when he knew Penny had once loved Dick?

"I was merely characterizing your charming friend, the alluring widow. She is a cat. She purrs and purrs, then darts out her claws and digs. She—"

"You are speaking of your guest. Remember?" His usually laughing eyes were stern.

"I know, Geoff. I—I shouldn't have said that. But, oh, everything is so mixed up and horrid and—and hopeless." She turned her head away with a little sob.

His hand dropped to her shoulder, gave it a brotherly pat. "What's the matter? Wires crossed? They get that way sometimes in life. There come hours with us all when things seem to be an infernal mess and tangle, but, good Lord, they invariably straighten out. Things have a marvelous, unbelievable way of straightening out. Hold tight to that thought."

"Thank you, Geoff," she said huskily.

"Here you are!" Don's voice was icy. "Some of our guests are leaving. You are forgetting your duties as hostess, Penelope." He turned to Jarvis and the latter was taken aback to see the unveiled hostility in his eyes.

"Thank you for comforting my wife."

"Com—"

"You are the second man I've seen do it this afternoon."

"Don!" Penny scrambled to her feet with a cry of protest. "Don, how could you—I—I hate you."

His eyes looked down at hers, as frosty as a deep freeze. "I know that," he said.

XI

After Penny's outbreak she turned with a sob and ran across the lawn toward the house and the departing guests. For a few moments there was silence between the two men, tense and strained.

The man in the wheelchair was the first to break it. "Considering," he said, striving to keep his voice light, "that you and I have been friends for fifteen years, that comment of yours was way out of line, Don." When his friend made no comment he added sternly, "Whether you were attacking my trustworthiness or Penny's."

Donald Garth stood with his head bowed in thought, his white jacket making him seem taller in the dusk. Geoffrey Jarvis noticed with concern the lines that were beginning to appear in his face, the tightness of his mouth.

"To suggest that I am offering sympathy to your wife

69

behind your back is bad enough," Jarvis went on. "You practically throw an old friendship out of the window when you do that."

"It wasn't you," Garth was stung to reply. "I said it was the second time this afternoon. Not over a quarter of an hour ago I found Penny in Dick Wentworth's arms—"

"She may have been in them but what makes you think it was by choice?"

"Because," Garth answered, goaded beyond endurance, "Penelope married me, loving Wentworth!"

"I don't believe it. What on earth makes you give credence to an idiotic thing like that?"

"She told me so," Garth answered simply.

The silence was long and heavy this time. Then Jarvis shook his head. "There's something all wrong about this."

Don laughed shortly. "You're darned right there is something wrong."

"No, I don't mean that. Penny and Wentworth—uh-uh —it's impossible. She sees too clearly, too steadily. She'd never really love a professional Romeo. Oh, she might have been flattered, even infatuated for a time, with a guy like Wentworth, but that's all. No, Don, you're off the track somewhere. Anyhow, your attitude toward Penny—autocratic isn't the word for it."

"You may be right," Garth said wearily. He pulled a white garden bench near to the wheelchair and sat down, his lean strong hands clasped around one knee.

"I know I'm right."

"Penny says she didn't ask Wentworth here. She thinks Kitty did."

Jarvis was puzzled. "That doesn't make sense," he said flatly. "You remember how Mrs. Owens practically ordered Wentworth out of her house, refused to admit him, and called him a fortune hunter. Kitty had no use for the fellow either. And the way he carried on when she married Tom Scarlet, as though Scarlet had robbed him of Kitty's money. It was a disgusting exhibition. No, I can't believe Kitty would ask him to Uplands." He moved in the wheelchair, trying to make himself more comfortable.

"How's the leg?" Don asked anxiously.

"A bit uncomfortable. It aches because I've been sitting up too long, I guess."

"That accident was meant for me, you know," Garth said. "I haven't told you how sorry—"

"Skip it. But that brings up a point that bears on our little

70

disagreement. When I was smashed up and knew that I couldn't keep an eye on you any more, I told Penny enough about the situation to put her on her guard, so she could carry on in my place."

"She told me. You had no right to do that," Don said hotly.

Jarvis held up his hand. His eyes were steady. "There is more at stake here than a woman's feelings," he said. "Or your feelings, for that matter. If your secret is learned by the enemy, the loss to this country, to the free world, is incalculable. That's the only point to keep in mind. I told Penny because she is more valuable than half a dozen armed guards. The men at the Works are crazy about her. The nursery school she is planning for their kids and those classes for their wives have made her tremendously popular. No one would harm a hair of Penny's head or stand by while someone else did it. So long as she is with you——"

"If you think I am going to hide behind my wife's skirts," Don began furiously.

"And the secret?"

There was a long pause.

"I wish," Jarvis went on, "you could have seen Penny when I told her, seen her eyes and the tilt of her chin and the ring in her voice when she promised to drive back and forth to the Works with you. There's something about that wife of yours——" He broke off and added gruffly, "You won't find many young women with such gay courage, such character. When she gave me her promise, nothing on earth would make her break it. That's why, when you come out with such an ugly accusation——"

"Sorry," Don said. "I owe you a deep apology. I mean that, Geoff."

"You owe it to Penny." As Don remained silent he added persuasively, "Why don't you tell her so?"

"You yourself heard her say that she hates me."

Jarvis laughed at him. "Can you blame her? The way you have been carrying on—like a Turk in his harem——"

A smile lighted behind Don's eyes, reached his lips. "I think," he said softly, "it is high time I tell Penny a lot of things I've been telling her only in my heart."

"It's like that, is it?" Geoff said.

"It's like that."

"Then why in thunder," Jarvis burst out angrily, "are you paying so much attention to Kitty Scarlet? Dangling around her all the time."

71

Don looked at him in surprise. "Attention to Kitty Scarlet? Geoff!" He laughed. "It's like that, is it?"

"It's like that," Jarvis admitted with a reluctant grin.

"We've been a pair of fools," Don said. "We seem to have been jealous of each other."

"I've been in love with Kitty for years," Geoff confessed. "I was all broken up when she married Tom Scarlet; though when he came in the picture I knew I wouldn't have a chance."

"What's wrong with you?" Don was indignant.

"That's not the question. What was right with Scarlet? He had qualities that have always fascinated Kitty: he was in touch with world affairs; he knew the secrets of nations. Kitty has always been interested in things like that. She's observant, keenly intelligent under that butterfly personality. And now——"

"And now she's free," Garth reminded him. "Why don't you tell her how you've felt about her all these years?"

"She——" Jarvis made a helpless gesture. "She's like a butterfly, lovely, frivolous, flitting about. I am afraid, Don, she wouldn't care to be a real wife. I've heard her marriage with Scarlet wasn't a success. Perhaps that was just gossip. Anyhow, she's been very gay since she became a widow. She's been seen everywhere, pictures in the magazines with the international set, all that. Doesn't seem as if she'd cared much for the man."

Don tapped his shoulder. "I hope it will work out for you," he said quietly. "I must return now to help speed the departing guests."

"Don," Jarvis began as Garth rose to his feet, "what is happening at the Works?"

Donald Garth thrust his hands in his pockets and stood frowning down at his friend in the wheelchair. "I don't know," he said heavily. "There's still a leak somewhere. But we can't trace it. A link in the chain of information somewhere that escapes us. Bits of fact are getting out. Of course, I am the only man who knows the whole thing but it is possible, I suppose—though not probable, thank heaven—that with time and patience enough, the enemy could piece together the entire thing."

"Are you positive that the blueprints of the new plane are safeguarded?"

"The blueprints are——" Garth paused. Caution intervened, even in dealing with his best friend. "They are safeguarded. Well"—he straightened his shoulders—"better have Macy

72

wheel you back to your room, old man. This has been a wearing afternoon for you."

Geoffrey Jarvis laughed. "The playboy," he reminded his friend, "is expected to have a social flutter once in a while."

"Playboy," Don chuckled. "If people only knew!"

ii

In the late twilight the family and house guests relaxed, lounging indolently on the terrace, and discussing the party. Only Terry, whose splendid youth and vitality knew no ebb, perched on the stone parapet, his legs dangling over the edge as he gazed off at the glistening bay to the south. The light from the rising moon seemed to concentrate on the white sails and dim bulk of a ship setting out for the open sea.

The moon, the moment and the mood fired the boy's dramatic ardor:

> "Sail on, sail on, O Ship of State!
> Sail on, O Union, strong and great!
> Humanity with all its fears,
> With all the hopes of future years,
> Is hanging breathless on thy fate!"

The rich boyish voice which had begun the quotation with theatrical exaggeration, steadied and deepened as line followed line.

"It doesn't seem possible," he said slowly, "that beyond that ocean there are people who want our ship of state to sink, who are trying, right now, to bore holes that will make it unseaworthy."

He turned to take a cup of coffee from the tray Fane was holding and the butler moved on, graven-faced.

Penelope stole along the terrace in the dusk. Her brother's eloquence, the beauty and the timeliness of the words he had repeated had been the last touch needed to set wide the floodgates of emotion. As she reached the French window which opened into Garth's study she looked back. She had left Don sitting near Mrs. Owens and she could still see the red glow of his cigarette like a firefly in the dusk. With a desire to escape from everyone she stepped into the quiet room.

"Who is it?" Penelope asked sharply.

A dark figure backed suddenly away from the desk and stopped.

"It's Macy, madam," a voice answered, as startled as her

73

own. For a moment she saw the valet silhouetted against the hall light and then the door closed behind him.

Penny stood looking at the door in perplexity. She remembered the words she had overheard in the garden: *Risky, very risky—no other way,* and Macy moving furtively through the hedge to avoid being seen. She must tell Don. No, she remembered, Don did not trust her. Then she would tell Geoff. Geoff would know what to do about Macy.

She groped her way in the darkness to the deep couch which stood at right angles with the fireplace. The soft cushions invited confidence. She buried her head in them, while a host of images went through her mind: Don putting Kitty's rose carefully away in his wallet *(Why did that hurt so?)*; Kitty making her mocking comment about Dick Wentworth's infidelity; Don's barely controlled fury when Dick had jeered at him in the garden, practically putting into words his knowledge that she had married him without love; Dick holding her in his arms, his triumph at the idea she had asked him to Uplands; Don dancing with her, sweeping her through heaven and then bringing her back to earth with a jolt by demanding to know why she had asked Wentworth to the house. And on top of everything else, though she had been blamed for a malicious action of Kitty Scarlet's, even Geoffrey Jarvis had turned against her, reminding her that Kitty was her guest.

Secure in the dim remoteness of the study, Penny let the tears come which had seemed to be choking her for hours. They came in floods. She was too engrossed in her unaccustomed indulgence to hear the hall door open or notice the figure which stopped for a startled instant and then walked quietly to the desk.

When the tempest had passed the girl sat erect with an apologetic laugh.

"There, Penelope Sherrod! You did it that time. That shower ought to suffice for years. It was tropically violent while it lasted. Get a grip on yourself, my dear, and remember what Geoff said." The admonition which had been delivered aloud had been punctuated by sobbing breaths.

"And what words of consolation did Geoff administer?" inquired a voice as the lamp on the desk flashed into light.

"Don!" The word was a gasp. Penelope blinked in the sudden light and made furtive dabs at her eyes with one hand while with the other she attempted to put her hair into place. "When—did you come in? I—I thought I was alone."

"Obviously. Do you indulge in this—this sort of thing often?"

"No, I do not!"

Indignation at his tone drew the girl to her feet. Impetuously, she crossed to the desk behind which he stood, like a judge behind the bench, she thought, watching her with dangerously cool eyes.

"I—oh, things just got too mammoth today for me and so I—well, I cried. I hate sodden women, too," she confessed with a flash of shy friendliness.

Garth steeled himself against the witchery of her eyes. "Penelope," he said, "why are things so mammoth? Is it because of Dick Wentworth?"

His face was white. The veins in his forehead stood out. The knuckles of the hand clenched upon the back of the ornate leather desk chair gleamed like ivory. The girl's face was as colorless as his.

For both of them the moment was a tense one, an inevitable sequel to the moment when they had stood face to face on the day of their wedding.

For an instant Penny wanted desperately to pour out her heart, to deny the hot words, "I hate you," which she had uttered a few hours earlier. She remembered how he had answered, "I know you do."

"Is our marriage any more of an obstacle to me than to you?" she demanded passionately. Before he could reply she went on, "I told—told you when we were dancing that—even if you could not love me you could trust me. I didn't ask Dick Wentworth to Uplands, Don. When he—when you and Mrs. Scarlet—that scene in the garden," she added incoherently, "it wasn't my fault. I told Dick I didn't love him any more. Only he wouldn't believe me."

Garth took a step forward and seized her hands. His eyes bored into hers. His face glowed. "Was that true, my—Penelope?"

"Yes. I wanted to tell you weeks ago. It seemed only fair that you should be told. But I didn't know how. And then—"

His hands closed tighter and tighter over hers. "Tell me."

"Then I realized—the day we were married when Dick talked as though marriage—didn't matter—that I couldn't love him. I was—I was ashamed to think I had ever believed he rated loving."

"What does marriage mean to you—and loving?"

"Marriage," Penny said promptly, "is a union—forever. It means loyalty, unalterable trust. It means a partnership, a sharing. And love—" she brushed her hand across her eyes —"means—"

"Happiness?"

"That, of course, but not just that. A flame and a delight, a deep warmth, sacrifice, if necessary. Pain and suffering, if necessary. But—" she finished simply—"all you have in the way of feeling, I guess."

"Why didn't you tell me before," he asked hoarsely, "that you no longer are in love with Wentworth?"

"Because I thought it didn't matter to you. And then— Kitty came. And—and anyhow—" Penny was so breathless that she could not finish.

His arms gathered her to him, he bent over her. "Anyhow?" he prompted her softly.

"Anyhow," she said, "you are so cold—so—so—woodeny that—"

With a stifled exclamation Don lifted her face, his eyes shining. "You've called me cold and woodeny before!"

He kissed her eyes, her hair, the dimple in her chin, her white throat. His face was colorless, his eyes blazed dangerously as he released her.

"Well?" he challenged. "How will you have me? Woodeny or—or like that? You will have to choose. There can be no middle ground for me."

It was true. This was no schoolboy, it was a determined man she had to reckon with. A man who stirred her more than Dick Wentworth had ever done. Penelope's hand was at her throat. Her long lashes hid her eyes. She swayed toward him with a lovely, unconscious gesture.

And outside the French windows Kitty exclaimed in a tone of cool surprise, "Macy! What in the world are you doing here?"

Don stiffened, turned toward the French windows and the woman outside. Penelope's eyes flashed for a moment to his white face. He seemed to have forgotten her.

"I am sure that I prefer you woodeny," she announced with ineffable scorn.

Without a word, Garth released her, strode to the open French windows and stepped out on the terrace to join the young widow.

XII

The telephone call came early in the morning. Penny had been dancing with Don, swaying in time to lovely lilting music. They were dancing on a rose-tinted cloud. And the telephone bell jangled, the dancing stopped, and Penny reached sleepily for the phone beside her bed.

"Mrs. Garth?" The voice was so muffled by excitement and haste that Penny found it hard to make out the words. At last, through the confusion, she disentangled the idea that Private Terence Sherrod had been injured during target practice at camp. She was to come at once.

With fumbling fingers that seemed to be all thumbs Penny dressed in a soft green suit with a tailored blouse, a tiny green hat on the back of her head. She started for the door, came back. Scrawled a brief note of explanation for Don and one for Nora. She gathered up handbag and gloves, propped the notes conspicuously where the maid would be sure to find them, and fled toward the car.

As she started the motor she thought, with a pang, of her promise to Geoffrey Jarvis, her promise to guard Don. But surely—just this once—he would be all right. Anyhow, what else could she do? She could not refuse to go to her injured brother and, judging by the excitement in the voice over the telephone, he must be seriously hurt. Perhaps—she shook her head to drive away the thought—she would not allow herself to think of that.

Usually a conservative driver, she sent the car roaring along the highway, watchful for the state police. She must not be stopped now. If Terry's injury were serious—

She glanced at the dashboard clock. Only six-thirty. She might still be able to see Terry and return in time to take Don to the Works. After the unaccustomed afternoon of leisure he had taken from his office to play host at the garden party, he would probably have arrears of work to make up. Since Kitty's arrival he had not withdrawn to the study in the evenings. He had spent them being charming to his guests.

And Kitty—face it, Penny told herself—you are jealous of Kitty's loveliness, of the fact that she attracts everyone: Dick Wentworth, Geoffrey Jarvis, Don. Last night—just when things might have been straightened out between her and Don, Kitty had had only to speak outside the window and Don had forgotten her presence, had stood listening as though something vital hung on the words of the woman with the yellow hair.

Penny pressed her foot harder on the gas, fear for Terry growing in her mind. She tried to discipline it by putting her mind on other things. Panic would not help. The garden party, she thought, had been a great success, as well managed as clockwork, the food superlative, the music for dancing the best that could be obtained, the guests amusing and amused. If she had not provided Don with a wife, at least, she told herself defiantly, she had provided him with a hostess.

Her mind clung to the party of the day before, because it was less frightening than Terry's accident. There were moments that stood out, not forgotten because she had not yet been able to think them through. Macy, for instance, and the low-toned, furtive conversation behind the hedge. *Risky, very risky—no other way.* She should have reported that conversation to Geoff but he had been unexpectedly stern with her because she had criticized Kitty.

Kitty! What was there about the woman that made all the men so eager to come to her defense? She remembered Kitty's high trill of laughter when she had seen Dick Wentworth trying to make love to her, and Dick had turned away at once, had offered his arm to the pretty widow.

And Don—there was an unexpected pain around Penny's heart. Don had followed Kitty last night out onto the terrace, after he had held Penny in his arms, after—for one breathless moment—

A car roared down the road behind Penny at a terrific pace, sounded a horn, passed her with a whiff of wind, turned back into the lane in front of her, jammed on—

Penny, heart in her mouth, stepped on her brake to keep from crashing into the car ahead, saw she could not stop in time, turned the wheel hard, pressed her foot on the gas, zoomed ahead on the left, turned back onto the road, and behind her the car which had braked so suddenly lunged after her.

Penny, the wheel gripped hard in her hands, caught her breath. Her heart was racing. They tried to wreck my car, she thought. They are following me. What can I do? She was thinking clearly, her mind working on all cylinders. She was cool. She braked, made a sharp right turn onto a secondary road that was in good condition. In the rear-view mirror she saw the other car turn, follow her.

I made a mistake, she realized, with her first touch of fear. I should have stayed on the main highway. There's no way off this. They'll get me.

She came to a crossroads, turned left, heading back for the highway. Temporarily, around a turn, she was out of sight of the pursuers. The road wound ahead. No one would be able to tell in which direction she had gone. On her right there was an unoccupied summerhouse. She braked, turned into the driveway which circled the house, stopped behind the house, turned off the motor. Waited.

In a few moments the second car roared past. She waited until the sound of the motor had died away, started the car, was about to retrace her steps when she realized that within a matter of a few miles the pursuing car would have a clear view of the highway for a long distance. They would know she had sidetracked them. They would come back.

Don't be afraid, she told herself sharply. You've got to think and think fast. She got out of the car and ran to the garage. It was unlocked. She rolled up the door, backed the car in, closed the garage door and ran out toward the road. She crouched down behind a hedge to wait.

In a flash the whole thing came to her. That telephone call! If I'd used my head, she thought, I should have known at once. The army is an impersonal organization. They would never have telephoned so breathlessly, so excitedly, to tell me Terry was hurt. There would have been a calm, disciplined voice. Oh, what a fool I am! The whole thing is a plot to get me away from Uplands, to keep me from driving Don to the Works.

In that moment of blinding realization she forgot her own fear, her own precarious position. Don! It's Don who is in danger. They are going to do something to Don. I've got to get to a telephone, I've got to warn him. Don! Be careful, darling, be careful . . . Why, she discovered, in overwhelming surprise, I love him. I love him. It doesn't matter what happens to me. It's just Don.

In a few moments she heard the roar of the returning car, then it slowed down. Stopped. Her heart was pounding so hard that she was almost deafened by it, her breath came in great heaving, noisy gasps. She fought herself to breathe slowly, deeply, her heart steadied.

The car was only a few feet away. She could hear voices; at least, one voice, but she dared not lift her head to see the two people who were speaking for fear they would catch sight of her.

"She must have turned into one of the driveways along this road, waited for us to pass, and doubled back," said the voice. It was excited but low-pitched. There was a haunting familiarity about it but Penny, straining her ears, could not remember where she had heard it before.

The other person spoke so low that she could not catch a single word, could not distinguish even the tone of the voice.

The first voice spoke again. "No, that's one thing we needn't worry about. She can't telephone. There are only two farms with telephones and she passed them. The houses along this road are all unoccupied. The telephones won't be connected."

There was a murmur of sound, indistinct, muffled.

In answer to some unheard comment, the first voice said, "We can't hurry it. We'll lose her if we do. I know it throws our schedule off but we've got to get hold of the girl now, whatever else we do. If she manages to get back to Uplands and raise the alarm, the fat will be in the fire. Garth will be so well guarded from then on we'll never be able to lay hands on him."

So I've simply got to keep out of sight, Penny thought. Until they find me they won't dare go after Don. She clenched her trembling hands, then forced them to relax. I'll lead them a chase, she promised herself grimly. One foot was cramped and she shifted her position, making the hedge rustle. For a moment her heart was in her mouth. Then she reassured herself. They won't notice it. They'll think it is the wind. Her confidence was a trifle shaken when she realized there was no wind. It was a still morning and the sun had become hot on her head and the back of her neck.

The voices were silent now but the car had not moved. Go on, she told them in her mind, go on. But there was no sound at all. They had stopped talking. The motor had been shut off. Absolute stillness. Then there was the high sweet voice of a bird and the flicker of color which was a yellow butterfly. It rested for a moment on the green sleeve of her suit.

The bird rose with a startled flutter of wings and flew off. What had startled it, she wondered idly. There was a sound —a whisper of sound—beside her?—behind her?—and then something struck the back of her head. She saw the grass rising to meet her.

ii

Something banged at her head as though it were being

80

struck with hammer blows. Penny moved and a lancing pain went through her head and her eyes. She opened them. She was lying on the floor in the back of her own convertible, one cheek pressed against the rug. She was doubled up but a moment's experimentation showed that she was not tied.

She listened. Not a sound. Memory flooded back and with it a great fear. The men had gone—and Don? What were they doing to Don?

How much time had passed since she had been knocked unconscious? Had they had time to reach Uplands? Or had they stopped Don on his way to the Works? Had he driven alone? Would they mur—no, no, things like that couldn't happen!

She pulled herself up to her knees and her head fell against the back of the front seat while waves of darkness swept through her head, blinding her, leaving her shaken and dizzy.

Slowly, painfully, she opened the door. Crawled out of the car. She was in the garage, the door was still rolled down, but a small door at the side, leading to a breezeway that connected with the house, was ajar. She glanced at the dashboard but, as she had expected, the car key had been removed. They were taking no chances of having her escape.

Out of habit she started to slam the car door. Some instinct made her hesitate. She left it open, straightened up. She leaned against the wall of the garage, her legs buckling under her. When she moved, the pain in her head was almost more than she could bear. But she was driven on by anguish, by an uncontrollable fear. Don! Somehow, someway, she had to get a warning to him.

And then she smelled the smoke of a cigarette. Someone was near her! She stood motionless, listening, holding her breath.

"So what do we do?" asked the voice she had heard before —how long ago? She glanced at her watch. It was difficult to focus. She blinked her eyes, tried again. Ten o'clock! She had been unconscious a long time, nearly three hours. They must have heard her when she had changed position behind the hedge, crept behind her, knocked her out. But they were still here. Her heart leaped. There might yet be an opportunity to get a warning to Don!

Only how was she to do it? How was she to make her escape? They had taken the key to the convertible. Anyhow, she could not have rolled up the big door of the garage and started the car without being heard. They were only a few

81

feet away. She could never escape by car. And the only other exit led to the breezeway where the two men were sitting.

There was a low indistinguishable murmur, and though Penny listened with all her attention, she could not detect a single word. But the first voice—where, oh, where had she heard it before? It was maddeningly familiar. Like a strain of music one can sing from beginning to end and yet cannot identify by name.

"Kidnaping!" it exclaimed now, speaking louder in surprise. A muttered exclamation made him lower his voice. "That's what it amounts to," he said more cautiously. "Sure, Garth would come with ransom money to free his wife. We could get hold of him all right. We could even"—there was an ugly note in his voice—"get the information we want if we go at it the right way. But—"

The low murmur again.

"No," the first voice said, "that isn't all we want. Not by a long shot. At least, it's not all I want. I want to get out of this with a whole skin. I am not going to tangle with the FBI."

Curious how a voice can frighten you, Penny thought, when you can't hear a word it says. But there was menace in that low murmur. Unspeakable menace.

The first man laughed grimly. "Maybe. Just the same I am a lot more afraid of the Feds. I'll take my chances with anyone else—even—"

A bird fluttered for a moment in the dim garage. Where, Penny wondered idly, had it got in? Not through the door at which she was standing. Where—suddenly she was alert. She turned, saw the small window on the opposite side of the garage, a window that had been broken. Probably by children during the time the house had been shut up. Certainly the owners would never have left it like that.

She slipped off her shoes, carried them, went on tiptoe around the car. The window was not locked. She pushed it up, inch by inch, tossed her shoes outside, pulled herself up, wriggled, pushing, until she could thrust her head and shoulders out of the window. For a moment, with her head hanging down, she blacked out, almost fell, then she wriggled through, let herself drop on the grass, gathered up the shoes and ran lightly on the grass out to the road.

For the first time she felt a rising of exultant hope. The other car was still standing as the men had left it, doors open so that she would not be warned that they were creeping up behind her. *And the key was in the switch!*

She got into the car, let off the brake, and it rolled down an incline away from the house. Then she started the motor slammed the doors, threw the car into gear and pressed her foot hard on the gas.

As she roared off she heard a startled cry and the thud of running feet, racing down the gravel driveway. No time to see who her captors were. They had the key to the convertible. Within two minutes, one minute, they would be behind her and now they had the more powerful car. She took a curve on two wheels, straightened the car, roared down the road at sixty, seventy, eighty miles an hour.

They were coming! Behind her she heard the roar of a motor, an insistent horn. She was sobbing now as she tried to get more speed out of the unfamiliar car. Another car had drawn even with her. A voice yelled. Penny moaned in her throat. She was caught. She put her foot on the brake, slowed down. Stopped.

She turned her head and saw an indignant state patrolman in his car.

With a cry of joy and relief she turned to him, talking so fast he could not understand her.

"I don't want to hear any alibi," he said sternly. "Do you know how fast you were going?"

"I was running away."

"I'll say you were. License?"

"I haven't got it. It was in my handbag."

"No license." He wrote laboriously in his little book. "This your car?"

"I don't know whose car it is."

"Stolen car." He wrote again.

"Please, please, listen to me," Penny cried desperately.

"Name?"

"Mrs. Donald Garth," she said. "Oh, please, officer, please! I was kidnaped."

For the first time he looked up from his book into the face with the bruised and scratched cheek, the wide, frightened eyes. He listened while she told him rapidly, trying to speak clearly, not to waste precious moments, what had happened.

"That the Donald Garth of the Garth Airplane Works?" he asked, interested in her identity.

She nodded and clutched at her head as a lancing pain went through it at the unguarded movement. "Please hurry. Please. They have my car. A cream-colored convertible. License—" she gave him the number quickly. "Look," she cried suddenly. "Behind! That's my car. Oh, they've seen you. They are making a U-turn. Hurry! Hurry!"

The officer backed, turned, started in pursuit. But the cream-colored convertible was already out of sight.

XIII

Garth's expression was formidable as he frowned down upon the chauffeur at the wheel.

"Good morning," he said curtly. "Why are you here?"

The man touched his cap. "Mrs. Garth left orders that I was to take you to the Works and call for you, sir, if she didn't get back in time."

"Didn't get back? Where has she gone?"

"She left a note, sir." The chauffeur handed it to him. "Nora says someone sent word from camp that Mr. Sherrod had been injured."

"Oh, I'm sorry to hear that. Well, you may go back. I'll drive myself."

The man's honest face was red with protest, his mouth stubborn. "Sorry, sir. Mrs. Garth insisted. I don't know how I could face her, sir, and say as how I'd let her down."

The gravity vanished from Garth's eyes. For a moment they were alight with fun. "Insubordination! Come out now. Step lively!"

The man's eyes were steady. "Only if you fire me, sir."

For a moment Garth was surprised, then he nodded. "Carry on," he said. 'I give up." He got into the back seat, thinking of the loyalty which Penny inspired in all the servants. Out of the corner of his eye he saw someone move as the car swept around the driveway.

"What is Fane doing at the garage at this time of day?" he asked sharply as the butler appeared between the shrubs, hesitated for a fraction of a second when he found himself observed, and then made his way to the service end of the house.

Over his shoulder the chauffeur commented, "He comes down every morning, sir." He added more slowly, "For a breath of air, he says."

"Oh, he does! After I leave Uplands, or before?"

"Why," the man thought slowly, ruminatively, like a cow chewing its cud. "Why, I think it's most generally before, sir.

I bring the car up for Mrs. Garth every morning and when I get back I usually find him in the garage."

"I see. Does he seem particularly interested in my plans for the day?"

"Not especially, as far as I've noticed, sir. He's a queer sort of chap. Very friendly. Don't say much, though. He mostly just sits outside the garage in the sunshine. Come to think of it, he does use the phone."

"Oh, he does. Do you know to whom he talks?"

"Couldn't say for sure, sir. Mostly just a few words. Sometimes I think he's checking the time with someone as he usually mentions it."

"Does he indeed?" Garth said softly. After a moment's consideration he added, "I don't need to warn you not to mention this conversation."

"Oh, no, sir!" the chauffeur exclaimed.

Garth's brow furrowed as he thought of Fane's peculiar behavior. He'd mention it to Geoff when he returned to the house. Obviously, Fane was reporting to someone on the time when he left the house each morning. It would be highly instructive to discover to whom the butler was making his report.

Curious how he missed having Penny beside him in the car. Her slim hands competent on the wheel, her eager eyes steadfast on the road. Lately, too, the wall between them had been crumbling and, as they drove to the Works, there had been gay talk and laughter between them.

Garth opened the little folded note. *Don,* he read, *I've been called away because Terry has been injured at camp. I'll be back as soon as possible. Don't drive yourself to the Works, please. And be careful. So much depends on you. Penny.*

He folded the note, lifted it to his lips, and put it carefully in his billfold. He found the faded rosebud Kitty had given him and, with a smile, tossed it out of the car.

He hoped Terry had not been seriously injured. Penny loved her mother and brother so deeply that she would be permanently hurt if anything happened to either of them. He remembered the sacrifice she had made in marrying him to save her mother.

Sacrifice! And yet there had been moments—no, there was no use hoping. He recalled her voice while they were dancing, her words after he had caught her in his arms and kissed her with the stored-up hunger of many weeks.

"I am sure that I prefer you woodeny!"

His mouth set grimly, but the human heart must hope and in spite of himself hope stirred again. For a moment Penny had melted into his arms as though she belonged there, as though she had found a refuge. For a breathless instant her soft lips had returned his kisses. Then Kitty had spoken outside the window.

Geoff had more than hinted that he was displaying too much interest in the widow. Perhaps—perhaps Penny was jealous. As he had been jealous of Dick Wentworth, even of Geoffrey Jarvis, who was his best friend. Thank heaven, at least, that Penny's love for Wentworth was dead. Her clear eyes had learned to see the fellow in his true colors.

The blood darkened Donald Garth's face and the muscles of his jaw tightened. It was ridiculous that real understanding between him and his wife was always being blocked by some minor interruption. They must talk things out. At least, she must know by now how he felt about her. Had he appeared to be cold and woodeny? Doubtless he had been, but there were limits to what a man in love could stand.

He remembered Wentworth's jeering comment at the garden party. Some day he and Wentworth would settle their differences in a final way. But why, why, in the name of heaven, had Kitty Scarlet asked the man to Uplands? It had been common knowledge that she had refused to marry him, that her mother had publicly dubbed him a fortune hunter, an adventurer. Kitty must know what sort of fellow he was. Then why? Why?

Of course, he reminded himself, Kitty was not like Penny. She was a gay and irresponsible flirt. Perhaps she was mischievous enough to enjoy stirring up her erstwhile victim into active admiration once more.

If that was the case he was sorry for Geoff, who loved her. What had he said—that Tom Scarlet had been able to provide her with the things she wanted, international affairs, state secrets. Don frowned. Those were not the interests of a truly frivolous woman. Was Kitty playing a part?

A thrush sang, the green leaves of trees in all their summer glory moved with a soft whisper. Gentle, musical country sounds. In a distant field a cow peered over a fence as the car went by. It was a peaceful, beautiful world. God grant that it could be kept that way!

The chauffeur's voice roused him. He had hopped down from the wheel and stood at the open door.

"You're at the Works, sir."

Garth emerged from his absorption in his thoughts. "Thank you," he said. "I must have been dreaming."

"I'll be back for you this afternoon," the chauffeur said. "Unless Mrs. Garth has returned by then."

ii

There were no free intervals during that busy day, a day in which he paid with interest for the time spent in garden party festivities, in which to think of his elusive wife.

He caught up with arrears of correspondence, signed innumerable papers, took countless telephone calls, made policy decisions with heads of departments, sat in on a meeting where faces were somber.

"There's still a missing link in the chain," one of the men said gloomily. "The blunt truth, Mr. Garth, is that we have tried and tried but we simply can't track it down. We know which country wants the plans for the plane. We've known every time men were planted here to get that information and we've picked them up when we wanted them. Others, about whom we aren't sure but have suspicions, are never really out of sight. We know where they go, whom they meet, how they spend their leisure, what their families and friends are like. The government is helping to do a superb job."

His closed fist hit the table. "But there is someone, somewhere, coming closer and closer to the vital secret. Whoever it is remains as invisible as a gas leak—and as dangerous."

The discussion waxed hot. Garth looked from face to face, grim, stern, determined faces. Not a man there he could not trust with everything he had, with his life if necessary. And it might come to that.

One of them introduced the subject bluntly. "There is no use in fooling ourselves," he declared. "Only one person has the whole thing at his finger tips; only one man can put together the jigsaw of facts and have the whole story. That's you, Mr. Garth. If they can't get the information any other way, they'll try to get you, to force that information out of you—"

"How?" Garth laughed.

"By torture, if necessary."

The ugly word hung in the room like heavy smoke. There was a long moment of silence while they thought about it, while their imaginations conjured up what it meant.

"It is impossible," the executive went on, "for any man to say how much physical torture he can endure. The mind breaks under it. A man may believe he would rather die than give any information that is demanded of him, but the time comes when he does not know what he is doing or saying."

Garth started to speak and one of the older executives broke in.

"I was here at the Works under your father, Mr. Garth. I don't need to tell you what we thought of him." He cleared his throat. "Or what we think of you," he added gruffly. "We can't have you fall into the hands of ruthless men."

The other man spoke. "In a way, the situation is fairly well covered. You are under guard constantly at the Works; Jarvis is keeping an eye on the situation at Uplands, although, of course, he can't do a lot with that broken leg except keep alert and check on the people who are in a position to get to you. He tells us that your wife is at the wheel of your car between the Works and Uplands. And I must say, Mr. Garth" —the man spoke with a new gentleness in his voice—"no one will ever dare harm Mrs. Garth. The men here—have you seen their faces light up when she goes by?"

Back at his desk after the meeting, Donald Garth leaned wearily against his chair. It had been a trying day and the mystery of the missing link of information that was getting out remained as much of a mystery as ever.

He glanced at his watch. Almost time to leave. There were only a few notes remaining on his desk to be handled. He always prided himself on leaving a clear desk and yesterday's accumulation had doubled his burden today. He went through them quickly until he came to the last, the one which must first have been laid on his desk the day before. A sealed envelope bore his name and the words: Private—Personal.

He tore it open.

Mr. Garth, he read, *there is a plot against you. Do not drive to work tomorrow. You will not be safe. Mrs. Garth will not be there for your protection. A friend.*

For a frozen moment Donald Garth stared at the warning. Into his brain were seared the words: *Mrs. Garth will not be there for your protection.*

Who could have known in advance that Terry would be injured? The call to Penny had been faked! She had been tricked into going away. She had been kidnaped.

He pushed back his chair so hard that it overturned, ran from his office like a madman, past his astonished secretary. Tore along the corridor to the outer door. No time to wait

88

for his car. He raced toward the parking lot where the employees left their cars. There was no key in the first one. On to another.

Footsteps pounded behind him. A man caught his arm. "Where are you going, Mr. Garth?"

Garth shook off the restraining hand. "Home," he choked. "My wife has been kidnaped."

"My car is always ready," the other said quickly. "This way, please."

Garth halted, studied the other man. "You are employed in the engineering department," he said.

A smile flickered over the man's face. "Only as a cover," he said. "I am the world's worst engineer." He pulled out his billfold, opened it, held it out to Garth. "I'm here to keep an eye on you."

"Then come on," Garth said hoarsely. "My wife—"

The car was old and looked as though it could barely limp along at thirty miles an hour, but miracles had been performed under the hood. Garth had never been driven faster in his life than on that ride to Uplands. Apparently, he realized, he was the only one not in the secret of the men who were guarding him, for several times state police cars started after the racing car and then, after a second look at the license number, let it go ahead unmolested.

The car turned onto the curving driveway, stopped at the door. Garth flung open the door before Fane could reach it. "Mrs. Garth?" he asked, gasping.

"She's back. Upstairs, sir." As Garth brushed past him, racing up the stairs, the butler called, "They didn't—hurt her badly, sir."

Fane did not notice the driver of the car who had followed Garth into the house. He moved noiselessly away to the telephone and dialed a number. The FBI man in the doorway listened to the dialing, checking each number in his mind. His eyes widened. He smiled to himself.

XIV

Geoffrey Jarvis lay on the big couch in Donald Garth's study, his broken leg stretched out. Penny had had Fane bring him there in the wheelchair for a conference; in any of the downstairs rooms of Uplands, in the garden or on the terrace, they were apt to be interrupted by Kitty Scarlet.

Penny had sent for him as soon as she had dialed the number of the Works and asked, heart thudding, whether Mr. Garth was there.

"He's in conference, Mrs. Garth," his secretary replied. "May I give him a message?"

"No—no," Penny said. "It isn't—necessary." She rested her head on her folded arms. Don had reached the Works safely. He was unhurt. He was all right. None of the nightmare things she had imagined had happened to him. Her relief was almost more than she could bear.

Geoff exclaimed in horror when he saw her scratched and bruised cheek, her clothes stained with dirt, her white face.

"Penny," he said, "have you been in an accident?" He added breathlessly, "Don?"

"Don is all right."

She poured out the story of the fake telephone message, the pursuit, the attempt to wreck her car, her escape from the garage when she had regained consciousness after having been knocked out. Jarvis listened, his face turning whiter and whiter.

"They weren't after me," she explained, "except as a means of getting hold of Don. They were going to send word to him I had been kidnaped and give him instructions for bringing ransom money. Then—they'd have him."

The telephone rang and she talked for a few moments.

"That was the state police," she explained when she had finished the call. "They found my convertible, abandoned. They will return it to me in an hour or so and they want to get more information from me. When I talked to that poor state patrolman—" She began to laugh. "Honestly, Geoff, it's no wonder the poor man was muddled. I was going eighty miles an hour where there's a thirty-five mile limit; I didn't have my driving license; I was in a stolen car. And before I could explain half of it my convertible appeared and I sent him tearing off in pursuit."

She sobered. "I told them I couldn't identify the men. I didn't see either one of them. Actually, I heard only one voice. The maddening part of it is that I *know* I've heard that voice before, Geoff, but I simply can't remember where."

"You heard only one voice," Geoff said slowly. "You didn't see either one of the people who were after you. Is that right?"

Penny nodded and then clutched her head as the movement sent a stab of pain through it. Why did Geoff look so odd? What had startled him so?

90

"Then," Geoff said, still more slowly, *"how do you know one of them was not a woman?"*

"Why," Penny gasped. "I don't, of course. I just took it for granted."

"You ought to be in bed, Penny," Jarvis said, alarmed by her white face, the shadows under her eyes, her colorless lips.

"I'm all right," she assured him. "Just a horrible headache from that blow on the head. Otherwise, I feel fine. As soon as I'd called the Works and knew Don was there and safe—" Her voice broke in a sob.

"At least, call a doctor and have your head examined," he said. "You may have concussion."

At his insistence she agreed but Jarvis was so frantic at the idea of her leaving the house, going to a doctor, for fear she would be captured again, that she asked the doctor to come to her.

"It's infuriating," Jarvis groaned, beating his clenched fists on the couch, "to be helpless like this just at the time when I am most needed. At least, you are safe while you are in this house."

"Am I?" Penny said oddly. She told him about Fane loading the revolver surreptitiously, watching her movements; about Macy and his furtive conversation behind the hedge during the garden party, and finding him in Don's study in the dark.

"Something is wrong with those two men, Geoff, I'm sure of it. Something is terribly wrong."

"Go to your room and rest," he insisted. "If Don sees you looking like that he will simply go out of his mind. He's so terribly in love with you."

Penny agreed, went to her room, and after the doctor had gone, shaking his head gravely and insisting that she be X-rayed the next day, she undressed with Nora's help. The nurse exclaimed and lamented over her, put turquoise blue lounging pajamas on the white-faced girl and opened the bed for her, piling up the pillows and putting an ice bag on the throbbing head. Penny winced as it touched the bruise.

"You go to sleep, child," Nora said. "And if those two men try to get in here they'll answer to me." She went into the small sitting room of Penny's suite and returned with the poker from the fireplace set. She settled herself in a chair by the bed, the poker clutched in her hand.

Penny lay back on the pillows, the ice bag tilted over her head, and closed her eyes. But she could not sleep. The pain in her head was enough to keep her awake and she was still profoundly shaken by her experience and too excited to rest.

She went over and over in her mind the sound of the hauntingly familiar voice, playing it as she would a record, but she could not remember to whom it belonged. The men who were after Garth must be close to her in some way. There was not only the familiar voice. But they had known about her brother, known that a call from the camp would send her flying.

Remembering that one-sided conversation, the determination to get Garth when he came to pay the ransom for her, she shivered. Don! Don! How long had she loved him so much that he blotted out all the rest of the world? How could she have been so blind as not to see what he was, what he meant to me? The thought of his face growing sterner and more remote after their marriage twisted her heart as though it had been squeezed by a giant hand. I did that to him, she told herself. How could I have hurt him so? And for what? For whom? For Dick Wentworth. Shallow, without honor, assuming I, too, had no honor. That once married to Don I would let another man make love to me.

She writhed with shame and Nora got up quickly, came to lay a comforting hand on hers, to say gently, "Does it hurt much, Penny—Mrs. Garth?"

Not my head, Penny wanted to reply. The pain is in my heart. She raised tired eyelids and smiled reassuringly at her old nurse.

"I'm not in pain," she said. "Just restless."

"I'll fix you some hot milk," Nora said. "No, I'm not going to leave you. I'll have someone else do it." She rang the bell and ordered hot milk from the anxious, wide-eyed maid who came to the door. The servants were in a state of high excitement. Mrs. Garth had left the house very early in the cream-colored convertible. Hours later, looking like death, she had returned in a strange battered-looking car and had been shut up with Mr. Jarvis for a long time. Now there was a rumor that she had been in an accident, that she was hurt. The doctor had come.

Penny sipped the hot milk obediently. The sedative Nora had slipped into it began to take effect. She heard Geoff saying, *He's so terribly in love with you.*

Don, she whispered to herself. She moved the hand bearing his wedding ring under her cheek. Don. She felt asleep.

Fane wheeled Geoffrey Jarvis's chair out onto the terrace where Kitty Scarlet sat in a bright-blue deck chair, wearing a sleeveless shirt and white tennis shorts, her gold curls fluttering in a soft breeze like a nimbus around her head.

"Talk to me, Geoff," she said with the imperiousness of a small child, and a spoiled child at that. "I've just come back from tennis at the country club and you've been neglecting me, you know."

In a moment Fane came out with tea things which he set before her. Geoff, watching idly, noticed that the butler, for all his deferential manner, was studying the widow in quick side glances.

Her eyes seemed even a deeper blue against the blue of the canvas chair. Lovely, frivolous, spoiled. Geoff sighed to himself. But so lovely. For all his efforts, he could not control the imagination that wondered to what lengths the frivolous curiosity, her love of excitement would carry her.

"Fane seems to be acting as nurse as well as butler," she commented.

"It's Macy's day off so Fane dressed me." Geoff laughed. "That's about all Nora leaves for anyone else to do. Penny is lucky to have her." He added thoughtfully, after a pause, "Especially now."

"A penny for your thoughts," challenged the widow gaily.

"I was thinking what a strange thing love is," he answered dreamily.

"Apropos of what?" The violet eyes touched his face, went on.

"Oh, nothing, nothing special. It seems such an infernally mixed-up thing, that's all. Nine times out of ten a man goes mad over a woman who is in love with someone else."

"Any particular case in mind?" she asked lightly.

"Yes," with a promptness and a glance which brought the delicate color to her face. "Here I am in love with you—have been since prehistoric times—and you—"

"And I?" she asked, and under the flirtatious tone she sounded alert, startled.

"Well, first," he said, "there was Tom Scarlet."

"Yes," she said softly, "there was Tom Scarlet. Two years of wonderful marriage, Geoff. In the beginning, after he died, I thought I could not bear it but then I found—other interests." She stopped abruptly, biting her red lips.

When he discovered that she was not going to continue, he said, "Will you marry me, Kitty?"

The violet eyes opened wide in genuine surprise. "Marry you?" she exclaimed.

"Why does it surprise you? I've loved you for years, and well you know it."

He was desperately in earnest. He meant it as he had never meant anything in his life and she was aware of the fact, aware of the tension in his hands gripping the arms of the wheel-chair.

For a moment it seemed to him that the gay face sobered, and then she laughed lightly. "No, Geoff, dear," she said. "It isn't possible."

"Is it Garth?" he asked her.

"Donald Garth!" For a moment he would have sworn that she was completely surprised. She laughed. "In love with Don? Heavens, no."

He leaned forward as well as he could with the cumbersome leg in its heavy cast. "Then why, Kitty? Why did you come here?"

She was evasive. "But I thought you knew. My Washington house is being remodeled and the town is so hot and crowded—"

He shook his head. "Not good enough. Think of a better reason."

A spark of anger lighted the violet eyes, made them smolder. "Don't be ridiculous," she said crisply. "I owe you no explanations for what I do."

He seemed to be unmoved by her anger. The tenderness in his voice was gone. His eyes were like steel, alert on her face.

"Did you ask Dick Wentworth to come to the garden party?"

There was a long silence and then she got to her feet. "Yes, I did," she said defiantly. When he made no comment she added, "What of it?"

"You didn't know, did you, that he had—that Don was jealous of him on Penny's account?"

"I discovered it—afterwards." She came forward a tentative step and touched his cheek lightly with pink-tipped fingers. "I am honestly sorry about that, Geoff. When Don and I came across Dick and Penny, with Dick trying to do his well-known caveman act, I was really sick about it. Don was so terribly upset. For a moment I thought he was going to knock Dick down." She added with a little smile, "I almost wish he had."

With a quick movement Geoff seized the hand so near his cheek, drew it to his lips, held it there in spite of her struggles to free herself. "Kitty—"

Unexpectedly she stopped pulling at her hand, let it remain in his. With her other hand she stroked his hair gently. "Geoff," she said, her voice soft, "you must believe me when I say that I would never do as your wife. I'm much too—too frivolous. If you had any suspi—any idea," she corrected herself hastily, "of the things I do, you'd be simply horrified. But I'm proud to think that you have loved me so long, even if I haven't deserved it. I'm honored to know you want me for your wife."

His hand tightened over her small one. "Kitty, look at me!"

Her momentary gentle mood had vanished and she made a gay *moue* of defiance as she obeyed.

"Never again," he said, "will you fool me. Never again will you get rid of me." He added laughingly but with underlying seriousness, "That's an ultimatum."

She pulled her hand away and evaded him when he would have detained her. All trace of emotion had left her face. It was tantalizingly gay.

"Geoff, darling," she laughed, "I want you to continue to be my faithful admirer. I need lots of admirers. I'd never be satisfied with just one."

She broke off to see her mother standing beside her. "Just in time for tea," she said gaily. Mrs. Owens settled herself in a deck chair and looked at her daughter with troubled, questioning eyes.

A car roared up the driveway. Don got out, raced for the front porch. Three pairs of eyes watched.

"What's wrong?" Kitty exclaimed. Her eyes were startled. She turned quickly toward the house. "What's going on here?" she demanded sharply. She broke into a run.

XV

Don had already disappeared. He ran quickly up the stairs, went to the end of the corridor to Penny's suite. The door stood open. He hesitated a moment, then approached and

95

looked into the sitting room. How dainty it was, how like its mistress.

On mantel, table and desk were innumerable photographs. Bookshelves lined one wall. Garth studied their contents curiously. There were shabby, well-worn volumes of poetry; there was a set of Dickens which looked as though it had done valiant service; there was Balzac limited and Kipling unlimited; there were a few of the modern French novelists; Jane Austen and Rachel Carson and Marchette Chute; and a profusion of books of reference.

As Garth looked at them he had the sense of having stumbled inadvertently upon an intimate family party, of having opened the door of the girl's mind without knocking. There was a simplicity and restful absence of detail in the room, the atmosphere of the place stole over Garth's tired brain like a benediction.

How little he really knew of Penelope's tastes. He had cared for her from the time she had returned from school, when she had made him feel as though he belonged to another generation. After they had become engaged—well, at least they had been good companions, he thought with a sharp sigh; but how far they had drifted apart since then. Had he been to blame?

And now, because she was his wife, she was endangered. He thought of the warning note on his desk, of the telephone call that had taken Penny away. Not badly hurt, Fane had assured him. Not badly hurt.

He tapped softly at the bedroom door and Nora opened it quietly, recognized him and came out, closing the door behind her. She still clutched the poker in her hand.

"She's asleep, Mr. Garth," she whispered. "I don't think she's much hurt. The doctor left a sedative and she's sleeping now, with an ice bag on her head because of the pain. They'll take X-rays tomorrow in case of a fractured skull but the doctor thinks it's just concussion and that she'll be all right."

He sagged against the door. "Concussion! Someone—struck her?"

Nora nodded. "A lump the size of an egg on her head. She wouldn't let me touch it because it hurts so."

"What happened?"

"A telephone call about Terry and not a word of truth in it. Mr. Jarvis has checked with the camp since then. He can tell you all about it because Penny—Mrs. Garth had a long talk with him as soon as she got back and had phoned the Works to make sure you'd got there and that you were all right. Though what she thought could happen to you I can't imagine. All I know is that she went out this morning before I was up, leaving a note about Terry, and came back a while ago in a battered-up old car, looking wild with excitement and half dead—there, I didn't mean to say that."

"May I see her? I won't disturb her."

"So long as you don't wake her up. She needs the rest—bad."

Don went into the bedroom and looked down at the sleeping girl, her face as white as the pillows, the dark shadows under her eyes, the scratches on her cheek, the bruises. And yet her mouth was curved in a tender smile. Her left hand was under her cheek. The ice bag tipped rakishly over her head.

He dropped to his knees beside the bed, his eyes resting on her face. Then he bent over and kissed her cheek, lightly, softly, and got to his feet. He stood, gazing down, thinking of the men who had struck her deliberately, who might have killed her. His face was hard as he passed Nora.

Still holding the poker the nurse went back into Penny's room without a word. Something in Don's stern expression made it impossible for her to speak to him.

As he reached the foot of the stairs the telephone rang. "I'll take it in my study," he said to the butler, who was hovering in the hallway. He went in, closed the door.

"Yes? . . . The state police? . . . I see. . . . I'd like very much to see you at once. Whenever you can get here. . . . Thank you." He put down the telephone and rang the bell. When Fane appeared he said, "Will you ask Mr. Jarvis to give me some time, please? If he can't come here, I'll see him in his own room."

"Mr. Jarvis is on the terrace with the ladies. I'll tell him."

In a few moments the butler reappeared, pushing Jarvis's chair.

While the butler was in the room, Jarvis limited himself to saying, "Glad you put in the elevator while your mother was ill, Don, or I'd be stuck upstairs in my bedroom. This way, I can move around as much as I like."

Fane started out. "Oh, Fane," Don said, "I am expecting someone from the state police. Please show him in here as soon as he comes."

"Yes, sir."

Don looked more closely at the impassive face of the butler. "Are you ill, Fane?"

"No, sir. Thank you."

He went out and Don raised his brows. "The fellow looks haggard. Maybe he's had bad news about his family."

"Didn't know he had a family," Jarvis commented.

"I don't know either. But something has gone wrong for him." Garth pushed aside the butler's problems. "Now, Geoff, tell me exactly what happened to Penny."

"She got a call about six this morning, saying her brother had been injured at camp and asking her to come at once. She left a note and started. She hadn't gone too far when a car tried to jam her off the road and when that didn't work— no, Don, she's all right. Anyhow, the convertible is a powerful car with a quick pickup and she got away, onto a side road, and then realized she'd be trapped.

"She turned into the driveway of an unoccupied country house, rolled the car into the garage and the other car went on. Doubled back when they found they had missed her. She heard them talking. They were going to kidnap her so that you'd come with ransom money and walk right into their trap. It was you they wanted."

"Did she see them?"

There was so long a pause that Don looked at his friend in surprise and repeated his question.

"No," Geoff said then, "but one voice was familiar. She never heard the other one."

"You say she recognized one voice?" Don asked sharply.

"Well, she felt pretty sure she had heard it before. Actually she couldn't place it but she may remember yet where she has heard it. She was pretty much dazed."

"Go on."

"She moved and gave herself away. They got behind her, knocked her out, and she regained consciousness lying on the floor of the convertible. She got out a window in the garage and escaped in their car. A state policeman stopped her while she was tearing along to warn you, and he went in pursuit. He called a while ago to say that he had found the convertible, abandoned, of course. That's all I know."

Fane opened the door and admitted two men, a stocky middle-aged man with a square face and observant eyes, and a tall good-looking younger man.

They introduced themselves. The older man was a captain of the state police, the other was the driver of the patrol car who had stopped Penny earlier that day.

"We've brought back your car, Mr. Garth, and we've checked the license number on the one in which Mrs. Garth made her escape. By the way, that was a very plucky thing she did. It took some quick thinking and a lot of courage. The car she was in was stolen, so there's no lead from it to the kidnapers. We'll have it checked for fingerprints. I understand from your butler that we can't see Mrs. Garth right now. As soon as we can interview her we want to get a description of the men from her."

Geoffrey Jarvis repeated the story he had just told Don.

"Then," said the captain thoughtfully, "the kidnaping attempt was made in order to get hold of you, Mr. Garth."

Don nodded grimly.

The captain leaned forward, his eyes intent. "Why?" he demanded.

"Because," Don told him, "we are secretly building a totally new kind of plane at the Works. That's all I am at liberty to tell you about it, Captain. The secret is not mine. But for some time there has been a leak. Each department knows only a certain amount. I am the only person who knows all the details. The danger, though it is not a likely one, is that, little by little, from information garnered in each department, they could piece together the whole picture. The chances, fortunately, are against it. So they want to get me in their hands and force the secret out of me."

"I see," the captain said. His face was set. He thought for a moment. "What steps have you taken in the situation?"

Don made a helpless gesture. "We have FBI men planted at the Works in the key spots, checking on the background of the employees who must necessarily know important facts."

The captain nodded. "That checks with our orders. There are some cars around here we are not to interfere with, no matter what they do. Well, what else?"

"Mr. Jarvis here, who—" Don grinned and for a moment the tired, harassed face looked younger—"who is not quite as idle a playboy as he appears, has been assigned to keep an eye on me at Uplands. Unfortunately," and the grin faded, "one of their attempts to get at me by tampering with the brakes of the car I usually drive got Mr. Jarvis instead, so he is laid up with a broken leg.

"My wife has been driving me back and forth to the Works because it was believed that no one would be willing to risk injuring her, but, of course, that's over now. That is one mistake we won't make again."

The captain looked to see whether the younger man had caught up with his notes. "Anything else you can think of that will help?"

"This," Don said. He took out his wallet and handed over

the note he had found on his desk a short time earlier. "I was supposed to find this yesterday but I didn't go to the Works because of a garden party we were giving."

The captain read it aloud: *Mr. Garth, there is a plot against you. Do not drive to work tomorrow. You will not be safe. Mrs. Garth will not be there for your protection.*

He folded it and put it away. "I'll keep this. Someone at the Works—" He and his companion got to their feet. "We'll do our best," he promised. "The car may yield a clue of some sort. But, if I were you, Mr. Garth, I would be mighty careful in the future. Don't be off your guard for a single moment. We'll put a man on full-time duty to watch you—"

"The FBI has already done that. He's going to take over the driving in the future. He's been masquerading as an engineer at the Works and from what he tells me, I hope he's a better driver than engineer."

"Fine. Just the same, you're in a nasty spot, Mr. Garth. For God's sake, watch your step!"

XVI

It was nearly midnight when Penelope opened her eyes. Because of the unaccustomed sedative she had slept all through the afternoon and evening. Now she was wide-awake. A night light was burning. For a moment she was bewildered when she saw Nora sitting in the chair beside the bed, the poker still gripped in her hand, head on her chest, fast asleep.

Penny was tempted to wake the older woman and send her to bed. But she knew Nora too well to attempt it. She would simply insist on staying where she was. No, it was better to let her sleep.

The movement of turning her head sent pain throbbing through it. The ice in the ice bag had long since melted and, with a cautious gesture, Penny took it off her head and dropped it on the sheet beside her.

Once more she relived her harrowing experience of the morning, up to the time when she had been knocked unconscious. Again she tried to force herself to remember where she had heard the voice that seemed so familiar. She recalled Geoffrey's startled comment, "Then how do you know one of them was not a woman?"

Too restless to lie still any longer, she got cautiously out of bed. At first her knees were so wobbly that she sank onto the nearest chair. She glanced over her shoulder at Nora, whose chair was drawn close to the bed on the other side, but the noise had not disturbed her. She was sleeping too heavily. Penny looked affectionately and in some amusement at her sleeping watchdog, then staggered to the chair across which the white velvet robe was lying and slipped it on, pushed her feet into turquoise scuffs and, hanging on to the furniture for support, because the floor seemed to have a curious way of tilting when she walked, she made her way out onto the small balcony where she stood, clinging to the railing, and looked down into the garden.

It was dark and still and fragrant, the perfume of flowers heavy in the air. Then a cloud drifted from across the face of the moon and the garden was filled with milky light. It became an enchanted place, so lovely that it brought a kind of sorrow with it.

In that unearthly glow, Penny allowed the love of which she had until now been unconscious to creep forth into the moonlight and watched it grow and grow until it filled the night. She leaned out over the balcony. There was no light in Don's study, no lights anywhere. Everyone must have gone to bed.

Moving noiselessly, she went back through the room and crept down the stairs, the white robe trailing behind her. She felt like a ghost of herself as she made her noiseless way, oddly light-headed, unreal, as though she were floating instead of walking. Perhaps, she tried to laugh to herself, to shake off the spell of the magic night, perhaps I'm really the ghost that haunts Uplands as some of the great English country houses are said to be haunted by unhappy ladies of the past.

Unhappy? But I'm not really unhappy. No woman can be unhappy when she loves so much. It makes the whole world bright, brighter than the moon. Even if I am not loved in return, it's the giving of love that counts. So on a summer night in June, Penny grew up and learned the secret of a woman's wisdom.

She went through the hall to the door which led to the garden, reached for the bolt, and discovered, in surprise, that the door was ajar. Even the impeccable Fane nodded at times. But how outrageously careless to leave a door unlocked at a time when Don was in danger!

Penny stepped outside and closed the door behind her. With a sense of freedom and adventure she made her way slowly along the path, keeping well in the shadow. The moonlight rioted over shrubs and blossoms. She stopped and looked at the marble girl in the fountain. How wonderful it would be to see her under the spray in this light. She dropped to her knees and struggled with the tap which turned on the water.

"Let me do that," said a voice behind her.

With a suppressed scream Penelope looked up into Donald Garth's face. Her voice threatened to desert her.

"Sorry," he said, his voice warm, tender. "I didn't mean to startle you."

He turned the tap and the fountain gushed on, flinging a shower of diamond drops high in the air to fall again in an opalescent mist.

"Oh, how exquisite," she said softly.

"Penny," Don said huskily, "I thought you were asleep and that Nora was guarding you."

She gurgled with laughter. "Nora is sitting beside my bed, holding a poker clutched in her hand, and sound asleep."

"But should you be up? The doctor recommended absolute rest and quiet until they make those X-rays."

"I couldn't sleep any more. Really I couldn't, Don. I've slept for hours and hours."

"How do you feel?"

She smiled reassuringly into his anxious face. "Fine. A little shaky, of course, and my head still hammers, but otherwise all right."

He growled in his throat and then his fingers, light as hummingbirds, felt the bruise so gently that he did not hurt her.

"Oh, Penny!" he groaned. "To have that happen to you, to have it happen on my account! Can you ever forgive me?"

His arms went around her, he drew her close to him. She could feel the thudding of his heart. She let her head rest on his shoulder. I feel as though I have come home, she thought. Warm, safe, protected. For a moment she leaned against him in sheer content.

His arms tightened. "Can't you, Penny? Can't you?"

"Can't I what?"

"Forgive me."

She laughed in sheer surprise. "How foolish of you, Don! You aren't to blame. How can you think I would blame you? As soon as I knew what was happening, all I cared about was"—her voice was fainter, muffled against his shoulder—"was knowing whether you were safe."

"Penny! My dearest." His head bent over hers; he kissed her.

102

Penny's arms lifted as of their own volition to go around his neck when he raised his head abruptly, dragged her back into the shadow of the shrubs, trying to stand so that he concealed the gleaming white of the long velvet robe.

She looked up, saw his eyes, wide and intent in the moonlight. She turned her head. There was the veriest ghost of a sound from the top of the wall that enclosed the garden. Every leaf on the vine-covered stones was visible in the moonlight. A hand appeared, then another.

A head was cautiously raised. Shoulders were outlined against the sky as a man drew himself up to the top of the wall, swung his legs over and dropped with a soft thud to the ground. He crouched there for a moment.

Garth held Penelope in a grip of steel while they watched, frozen, fascinated, the intruder who was creeping across the garden. From weakness, excitement and shock Penelope began to shake. She was not frightened. So long as Donald held her in the circle of his arms she could fear nothing. She opened her lips to speak and, though his eyes had not left the intruder, he seemed to be so aware of her that he knew intuitively what she was about to do. The fingers of one hand gently touched her mouth, pressed lightly, warning her not to make a sound.

The midnight visitor softly crossed the path until he stood beneath Penelope's window. She stifled a gasp of consternation. It was the draftsman whose dog she had saved. And she had thought him grateful! What was he doing here?

She lifted the restraining fingers from her lips and smiled up reassuringly at the man who was her husband. Unconsciously she clung to his hand as she watched the marauder. He examined the study windows and the French doors and then stood back to look up at the balcony that led to Penny's suite. Gently he tested the trellis that extended from roof to ground. He found a footing among the vines and pulled himself up a step.

Somewhere a door creaked on its hinges. The sound was intensified by the stillness of the night. With the agility and noiselessness of a panther the man dropped and disappeared through the gate which led to the garage.

Don drew a whistle from his pocket and blew shrilly. Almost at once it seemed to Penny that the garden was swarming with men. They came from everywhere. Don shouted instructions. Penny quivered with excitement.

"We'll get him," one of the men called. "You keep an eye on Mrs. Garth."

Don picked her up in his arms, carried her into the house

and up to her own room. He was nearly knocked down as Nora came charging out into the corridor, wild-eyed. She screamed when she saw Penny.

"What's happened to her? What's happened to her?"

"Nothing," Garth reassured her with a laugh. "I'm carrying her because she has had enough exertion for one day."

"I fell asleep," Nora was crying in her chagrin. "Oh, Mr. Garth, I failed you. I fell asleep."

"Never mind. You go to bed. I'm going to keep guard myself for the rest of the night."

When Nora had put Penelope to bed, Don sent her out to quiet Kitty, her mother and the servants, who had been roused by the turmoil in the garden and were asking excited, alarmed questions.

When the house was still once more, he settled himself in the chair Nora had occupied. To Penny's surprise he pulled a revolver out of his pocket.

"You can sleep and not be afraid," he said grimly. "I'll be awake all night."

Drowsily, Penny smiled at him, turned on her side, slept. For hours Don watched his sleeping wife, waiting for word about the marauder, waiting for the men planted both by the FBI and the state police to bring him in.

They did not find him.

ii

The following afternoon the garden slept in the sun. Bees and butterflies moved somnolently from flower to flower. The trees cast deep shade and their leaves moved in a gentle, sleepy rustle. The only sound was the distant throb of a power motor as a gardener mowed the lawn. It seemed impossible that the beauty and peace of this scene had been shattered the night before by running men, shouts, whistles, and tense excitement.

The shadows on the velvet green of the lawn at Uplands had begun to lengthen. A cool breeze gently swayed the treetops; oaks bent their stately heads condescendingly to the neighboring pines; the pointed leaves of the white birches fluttered flirtatiously.

Behind a thick planting of shrubs near the entrance to the garden a man lay hidden. His hand gripped the neck of the dog beside him. The animal dozed contentedly, its nose snuggled between its forepaws. One leg was clumsily bandaged. His master's eyes were dark and brooding as he kept them intently in a small opening in the growth before him.

Would she come? She must. He knew from having watched that she usually came into the garden at this time. He had failed in his attempt to reach her last night. The hours were flying. He must accomplish what he had come for and get away. There was no time to waste.

At any rate, there was no time for him. It was running out. Since the man who had been his friend had taken another to kidnap Mrs. Garth and so force Garth into their hands, he had known that he was no longer trusted. And when a man was no longer trusted, he was finished. There was no room in the enemy's book of rules for a doubtful man. They would kill him. Perhaps a shot from cover as he walked down the road. Perhaps a knife in the back. Perhaps poison in his food. The means did not matter. The end would be the same.

And even the end did not matter, he thought, lifting his head proudly. In the past men had died for their country on the battle line. In the modern world the battle must be engaged with the enemy wherever he appeared. A death without military honors, without medals, unknown. But, at least, his heart would be at peace. He would have done the best he could. No man could do more.

Petro did not feel sorry for himself or inclined to whimper at the ugly fate that awaited him. At least, he had a chance to atone for the folly of letting himself be caught up in the toils of the man he had mistakenly trusted. He stifled a moan, not for his own fate but for the fate of the brothers and sisters he had left behind in his country. Was he condemning them to death? He who loved them? Yet what choice had he? For the sake of people he loved he could not betray a principle. Men who did that cared more for themselves than for their world.

Petro had lived a whole lifetime in an atmosphere sometimes of vague and unknown menace, sometimes of clear-cut danger and imminent terror. He had never known, as he knew now, the strength that comes with a sense of unswerving purpose. He had never before been without fear for himself as he was now that he was offering his life willingly as a sacrifice. The man who does not fear death needs fear nothing, he discovered.

Would he have sacrificed himself so gladly, he wondered, if he had never seen Mrs. Garth? He closed his eyes and saw again the lovely girl who had stood beside the Chief at his drafting board, the glowing girl kneeling beside his dog, the warmth in her voice, the steady eyes of unlimited depth.

He confessed to himself that he did not know. He hoped that he would never again have to live through such mental agony as he had experienced when he discovered that the plan had been changed. Mrs. Garth was to be kidnaped so that her husband would bring ransom money and fall into their hands.

After that Petro knew what would happen. Torture until the mind gave way, the will was broken, and Donald Garth would give them information enabling the enemy to make the new airplane. And after that—of course, after that Garth would have to die to silence him forever, so that he could not identify the men who had tortured him for the secret.

Petro ran his hand through his hair. His forehead was beaded with perspiration as he remembered the growing horror with which he had waited for news of the outcome of the kidnaping. He recalled with a shiver the fury of that man, when he reported that Mrs. Garth had managed to slip out of their hands, that she had escaped and alerted the state police. No telling how much damage that abortive kidnaping had caused. The men behind the group who were after the airplane plans would not forgive such a blunder.

Petro remembered that the horror had begun for him when he promised to thank Mrs. Garth in actions rather than in words. He was a man who kept his promises, who regarded them as solemn obligations. When he realized that he was no longer trusted, he had pretended to be sick, left a note warning Mr. Garth not to drive to work and gone to the house of his "friend" to find out what was happening.

He had climbed through a basement window, worked his way slowly up to the first floor and crouched in a closet used for storing liquor in the room where the meeting was to be held. He had felt sure that no drinks would be served during the meeting. That was against their orders from overseas and these men followed discipline blindly.

He had listened avidly. He had heard that one of the men planted at the Works had succeeded in opening the safe in Donald Garth's office. The blueprints were not there. The new idea was to get the information from Garth himself. His wife was to be kidnaped. The meeting had been disrupted by the arrival of Petro's friend. The kidnaping had failed!

They were not men who lamented a failure. They went on to plan ahead. Garth had escaped them this time. The plans were not at the Works. Only one place remained—Uplands.

As soon as they had left, Petro had escaped from the closet and come to Uplands to warn Mrs. Garth. But someone had seen him and all at once the place was a bedlam of whistles, shouts, running men. He had barely managed to get away.

And now time was running out. "I've got to get to her first," Petro half sobbed to himself. "I've got to warn her. I can't go to the door or telephone or write. I must do it this way. I can't fail." His hands clenched. "I won't fail," he vowed.

His hand closed more tightly on Vag's neck. The dog opened one sleepy eye, yawned prodigiously, and with a sigh which quivered from his ears to the tip of his tail, relapsed into slumber. Then his head came up, his eyes widened, his nostrils dilated. The man beside him pulled him nearer and muzzled his mouth with steel-like fingers. The dog glanced at him reproachfully, snuggled closer and his eyes closed again. His manner seemed to suggest: If you won't pay attention when I warn you, my responsibility is over.

The tragic eyes behind the screening shrubs were keen as a ferret's as they watched the gate of the garden. A man entered, looked around. Petro was rigid, his breath rasping in his throat. And all at once he was afraid.

And then a woman came quickly through the gate, almost as though she were following the man. She stood watching him and then bent gracefully to gather a rose. She was small and fair and mischievously merry.

"Dick Wentworth!" she called gaily. She ran toward him.

He was resentful as he sullenly pulled at his small mustache. His voice was sharp with anger when he spoke. "Where on earth did you come from, Kitty? I am calling on Penny. I was anxious to know how she is."

The woman called Kitty turned to loosen her skirt caught on a thorn and for a moment her face was hidden. "Penny is fine," she answered. "But then she is always bursting with health. Haven't you ever noticed that wonderful color of hers?"

"You don't need to tell me how lovely she is."

"Why, Dick!" With a trill of laughter she pulled the rose through his buttonhole and stood admiring it, head on one side. "How you've changed."

He answered the mocking tone in her voice. "What does that mean?"

Her voice was unexpectedly sharp. "A few years ago you

found me lovely, so lovely, I believe, that you threatened to die if I didn't marry you. Or was it my money, Dick? Was it my money?"

There was amusement in his face. "No woman as beautiful as you, Kitty, needs to wonder why a man wants to marry her. Are you—is it possible that you are jealous of Penny?"

She laughed at him. "Not jealous, but very, very interested. There's a rumor going around that Penny would have married you like a shot before she accepted Donald Garth and you didn't make an offer. And now you begin to find her so strangely attractive you can't keep away. It wouldn't be Garth's money that attracts you, would it, Dick?"

Petro, watching from behind the hedge, saw the veins in Wentworth's temple swell. He was in a towering rage. He glared down at the malicious, mocking face. Behind the woman's big violet eyes there was cold steel. She was not the frivolous flirt Wentworth believed her to be. She was acutely intelligent and potentially dangerous. So dangerous that, for a mad instant, Petro was tempted to warn Wentworth that he was mistaken in her, to be careful.

Wentworth took hold of her arm, his fingers tightening brutally. "Kitty," he said, his voice shaking with anger, "I am in love with Penny. Love is a thing you could not even comprehend. It's a thing you will never attract. No man wants to marry a hummingbird. Perhaps it was your money, but it isn't Penny's. Penny is different."

She made no answer. Her lovely face seemed to be frozen.

"What do you intend to do?" he asked at length.

"I intend to interfere with your plans," she said quietly, and then she laughed, she was again an irresponsible butterfly. "But now I'll leave you to Penny. I hear her voice around the side of the house. She'll be here any moment." She went swiftly across the lawn and into the house through the open French windows that led to Garth's study.

Wentworth frowned as he stood looking after her. And then young Mrs. Garth came around the side of the house in a sleeveless white linen dress that set off her sun tan. Petro looked at her narrowly. Except for a slight bruise and a few scratches on one cheek she seemed to be uninjured. Though there were, he observed, pale shadows under her eyes. No, she had turned her head, lifting it to follow the flight of a cardinal, her eyes enchanted at the scarlet flame that soared for a moment under the blue vault of the sky. There was a bandage strapped behind her ear.

108

Then she saw Dick Wentworth, stopped short, rigid with anger.

Wentworth stood equally still, something moving behind his eyes as he studied her, as though asking a mute question. Then he went toward her eagerly, both hands out. "Penny!" he cried.

Her hands hung at her sides. Her chin lifted. "Dick, I told you once before," she said crisply, "that you were not to return to Uplands. Are you going to force on me the embarrassment of having to give orders that you are not to be admitted?"

His hands caught hers, lifted them to his lips. "Penny," he said, his voice breaking, "be a little kind."

The note of genuine feeling caught her off guard. It shook her anger, made her uncertain.

"But—"

"Why are you afraid to have me come?" he went on quickly. She snatched away her hands. "Afraid! Of all the conceited—let's have this clear, Dick. And I don't want to repeat it ever again. I am not in love with you. I am not in the least afraid of finding your presence disturbing in any way except by the distaste it causes me. I am unwilling to receive any man I can't respect. I—do—not—love—you. I loved you once, or thought I did, and you killed it yourself, Dick."

They had moved away and Petro parted the bushes, reckless of being detected.

"Then I'll resurrect it!" Wentworth's voice was hoarse with emotion. "You will love me again. Garth shan't have you." He seized her in his arms.

Penny struggled with him, her head pounding with pain as she fought. "Let me go," she panted. "Let me go!"

He bent over, kissing her wildly.

Petro jerked the dog to its feet. It was quivering with excitement. "At him, Vag! At him!" he said savagely.

With a growl the dog tore its way through the hedge into the garden. The watcher saw him seize Wentworth's leg. Then he stole stealthily away.

Hearing the menacing snarl, Penelope looked down. At the same moment, Wentworth released her so suddenly that she staggered and nearly lost her balance. Vag, the dog she had tended so devotedly, had come to her rescue. His eyes gleamed red as he took a tighter, deeper grip on Wentworth's leg. Dick's face was livid as he tried to beat off the dog.

He had lost in a hurry the world-is-mine expression he had

worn when he had grabbed Penny. She stifled a desire to laugh. She approached the dog and called, "Vag! Come here! Let go!"

The animal's teeth tightened for a moment, he shook his head, then looked at her, wavered, growled, and obeyed. He ran to her with a joyous yelp of greeting, and she dropped to her knees, her hand tight on his collar.

"You had better go, Dick," she warned him. "I can't hold him much longer."

Wentworth hesitated, savagely aware that he had been made to look ridiculous, a fool. Instead of conquering the girl, she was protecting him. Then, as the dog growled deep in its throat, he turned and went out of sight. Penny noticed that he was limping and she could not find it in her heart to be sorry.

She bent over the dog, patting it. Then she noticed the clumsy bandage on the leg. With deft fingers she unfastened it. Her brows met in a puzzled frown as the bandage fell on the lawn. There was nothing whatever the matter with Vag's leg. Then she saw a tiny slip of paper that had dropped beside the bandage. She drew back and stared as though it were some malignant thing. Her heart pounded with excitement as she picked it up and read the few words written on it: *Great danger for Mr. Garth. For God's sake meet me at icehouse. Hurry. I am suspected. Don't talk to anyone before you see me or I'll be killed. Your friend, Petro.*

That was all. The girl's brain reeled, then steadied. She had helped Vag and Vag's master was paying his debt. He must have tried to get the message to her last night. That was why he had attempted to climb the trellis to her balcony. Not robbery. Not something worse—another kidnaping. A glow of happiness warmed her heart. He must have sent that warning at infinite danger to himself. She must safeguard him as far as possible.

She glanced at the windows that overlooked the garden before surreptitiously tearing the paper into tiny scraps and slipping them into the pocket of her dress. She rebandaged the dog's leg, being careful to make a neat job of it as a kind of answer to the dog's master. Then she gave it a sharp pat.

"Go find your master, Vag. And tell him—thank you."

She got to her feet, watching as the dog worked its way into the shrubbery and disappeared.

She heard breathing behind her and turned with a start. Fane was close to her, his eyes, like hers, on the shrubbery.

"The men from the state police are here to see you, madam."

Penny thanked him. As she turned away she saw his eyes rest on the bandage on her head. There was a queer expression on his face.

XVII

Penelope's mind was in a tumult. Instinctively, she believed in the young draftsman who had sent her the message. She knew, without knowing how she knew, that he was genuinely to be trusted, that he was really trying to help her. He knew where the danger lay but, if she were not terribly careful to protect him, he might be killed before he could speak.

Hurry, he had written. But she could not go now. The state policemen were in the house. If she were to disappear at this time there would be a commotion. A search party would be sent out. And yet it was essential that she should reach Petro as soon as possible, reach him before he was found by the men who were seeking him.

Slowly she returned to the house, wondering what she ought to do. Icehouse, he had said. That must be the old abandoned icehouse a mile down the road. It had not been used for years. A good place for a secret meeting. But what about the state police? Should she tell them?

Don't talk to anyone, Petro had warned her, *or I'll be killed*. Don't talk. Don't talk. She could not afford to take that risk. He would not have warned her if he had not known that someone at Uplands was not to be trusted.

Someone here. Someone in Don's house. An enemy under his own roof. As she stepped out of the sunshine into the cool hall Penny felt a kind of chill that made her shiver. A feeling of foreboding. As though this house, which she loved, held some menace, threatened her.

I've got to keep my head, she told herself. She stood waiting, taking long deep breaths until she was quiet and relaxed. Then she went into the small morning room where the two men were waiting. She smiled and held out her hand to each of them.

During the interview that followed, she thought that she had never before suspected her own capacity for discretion, for dissimulation. She talked, answered questions, and all the time she was thinking of Petro's words: Danger . . . Don't talk . . . I'll be killed. She must guard her words, be careful that not a hint should escape her about the young draftsman. Someone here at Uplands might be listening, might hear her and track him down before she could reach him.

She described in detail the faked telephone message that purported to come from the army camp, and the attempt to wreck her car. She told how she had hidden it in the abandoned garage, and overheard the conversation of the two people. She explained how she had finally escaped from them.

The older man took her over and over the conversation she had heard.

"You say you heard only one voice?"

Penny nodded and instinctively her hand went to her head as it throbbed in response to the motion.

The police captain observed her gesture. He observed a great deal in an unobtrusive sort of way, Penny thought.

"I checked with your physician," he said. "I was delighted to learn that X-rays show there is no skull fracture, although he tells me you have a slight concussion and that you are suffering from shock. I must say, Mrs. Garth, you behaved in a very cool and plucky way. You did some nice, quick thinking when you made your getaway."

"When I realized they were after my husband," Penny said crisply, "I forgot to be afraid. I was so—so darn mad. All I thought about was warning him."

The two men smiled in quick sympathy and with a glint of admiration.

"I never," Penny declared, turning to the younger man with a laugh, "was so glad to see anyone in my life as I was to see you. I thought they had—" her breath caught for a moment—"I thought they had caught up with me again. And then I saw your uniform!"

She turned to the captain with a spark of her old gaiety. "First he found I was speeding and then I didn't have a license and finally I was driving a stolen car. Both of us were nearly crazy by the time we got it all straightened out."

The captain smiled at her. "Now to get back to the one voice you heard. Mr. Jarvis tells me you thought it was familiar."

Penny started to nod, checked herself, said, "Yes, I am sure I've heard it. The voice was distinctive and so familiar I feel I've heard it often. But I can't—I simply can't remember where."

"Don't worry about it," the captain advised her quickly. "And don't try to force yourself to remember. The concussion may have something to do with it. And then it may simply be because it is a voice you find it difficult to associate with a criminal, your mind balks at making the association. It's too far out of context."

"I don't understand," Penny admitted.

"Well, it's like—" The policeman sought for a comparison. "For instance, meeting in the seat next to you at the opera the boy who greases your car. The face will be familiar but the association is so different that it takes time to remember where you have seen him before. But if you were to meet him in a strange garage you'd know him at once."

"I see," Penny said. "I'll try not to think of it and perhaps it will come to me of its own accord."

"Or perhaps," the captain said grimly, "you will hear it again."

She looked at him with unwavering eyes but the color drained out of her face.

"Sorry," he said, "I didn't mean to frighten you."

"You didn't," she assured him, though there was a betraying quaver in her voice.

"Or perhaps," the captain said gravely, "perhaps I did. You must be on the alert, Mrs. Garth. Constantly. If you should hear that voice again—perhaps hear it in someone close to you—*don't betray the fact that you recognize it.* Your safety may depend on that."

"I—see." The girl's voice was faint but it was steady now.

"We'll keep an eye on you," the captain said as the two men rose to leave. "But don't believe any more telephone messages and don't go off anywhere by yourself. Anywhere."

The younger man laughed. "If you'd seen her face when I caught up with her, you'd know you would not need to tell Mrs. Garth that, sir."

This time Penny did not dare risk letting her eyes meet his. For one moment she longed desperately to tell these two men about Petro's message, to ask for their help and their advice. But they would not let her keep the appointment and she must go. She must go by herself. For Don's sake. And Petro had said, *I'll be killed.* She must not take that chance.

She said cautiously, "I'll be very careful, Captain." That, at least, was not a lie.

"You must be careful. Last night, judging by reports, you had another near escape. One of the fellows tried to get into

113

your room and then escaped. You see, they haven't given up yet, Mrs. Garth. They may try again."

But the danger, she wanted to cry out, is inside the house. Someone here. How can we be protected against that? Against someone we can't lock out?

"There seemed to be a lot of men all of a sudden," she said, "after my husband blew that whistle."

"There were. But even so, if Mr. Garth hadn't happened to be outside at the time, hadn't seen him, he might have got away with it. We'll try to pick these fellows up as quickly as possible. But, meantime, don't do anything rash."

Don't do anything rash. The words rang in Penny's ears after the two men had left. Fane, after seeing them out, returned to ask her where he should serve tea.

"On the terrace," she decided. "Will you ask Mrs. Scarlet to pour? And please make my excuses, Fane, and ask them to have tea without me. I must rest until dinnertime."

"Yes, madam."

I'll have two hours, Penny thought. Surely I can get to the icehouse and return in two hours. I'll be back while it's still light. There won't be any danger.

But she had counted without Nora. When she reached her room Nora scolded her fiercely for going out and forced her to lie down. She refused to listen to Penny's frantic protests and the girl knew the older woman too well to attempt to go out. Nora would simply stop her.

She lay down, thinking feverishly of Petro waiting for her, wondering why she did not come. Now she would have to wait and slip away after dinner. By that time it would be dark. No use thinking of it now.

The danger lay at Uplands, in the house itself. But who? Don, Geoffrey Jarvis, Kitty Scarlet, Mrs. Owens, Nora, Fane, Macv, the housekeeper, chauffeur, cook, housemaids. She considered them one by one. Geoffrey Jarvis was a government man, she could eliminate him. Kitty—she paused there. She thought of Geoff's words: *Then how do you know one of them was not a woman?*

She smothered a giggle as she tried to imagine Kitty as part of a gang. Maybe I'm green-eyed, as Nora says, but I'm not insane, she decided. No, Kitty could not be involved. Nor could her dignified mother.

Fane—she thought about the butler for a long time. If it's anyone at Uplands it must be Fane, she decided. I wonder why Geoff hasn't done anything about getting rid of him.

At length, Nora laid out a strapless dress of rose nylon

114

tulle and Penny started to slip it on. Thought of the trip ahead in the night to the icehouse. Put it away. She looked through her wardrobe and took out a black net dress, more sophisticated than those she usually wore, but one that would have the advantage of invisibility in the dark.

The dark! She looked out of the window and thanked heaven for daylight saving. If they could just hurry dinner a little she could still meet Petro and return home before it was completely dark. The nearer she came to the trip to the icehouse the less she liked it. She wondered what the policemen would say if they knew what she was planning and decided that she could guess.

When she was dressed she thought of going to the study, asking for the jewel box. But if she were in any danger, jewelry would add only another hazard. She slipped on the brief brocaded jacket of Chinese red that topped the dress, matching shoes, and went down to greet her guests.

At the insistence of the police no publicity had been given to her accident nor had the members of the household been told anything except that she had had trouble with the convertible. She did not know how last night's turmoil had been accounted for.

Don, looking taller in his white dinner jacket, turned quickly as she entered the drawing room. It was the first time she had seen him since he had settled himself beside her bed the night before, the ugly-looking revolver in his hand. When she had awakened that morning he was gone but beside her pillow lay one perfect rose and a scrawled note: *Take care of yourself today, my darling. You are very precious to me. Don.*

All day long that note had warmed her heart. It added now to her determination to meet the draftsman, to protect her husband if she possibly could.

She answered his smile radiantly, greeted Kitty and her mother gaily, asked about Geoff, who was not coming down to dinner because it was so difficult to manage his wheelchair at the table.

"What on earth was all the excitement last night?" Kitty exclaimed after they were seated at dinner. Fane, who was serving the soup, started and some of the hot liquid splashed over the edge of the plate.

"A housebreaker," Don said briefly after a warning glance at Penny.

"Heavens, did he steal anything?"

"Oh, no, he didn't even get in the house. I saw him and whistled. The chauffeur ran after him."

"Where on earth did you get that police whistle?" Kitty laughed. "When I heard it I thought the place had been raided."

"I picked it up as a joke," Don said casually. "Never expected to use it."

The idea of Don accidentally carrying a policeman's whistle in the pocket of a dinner jacket was so patently absurd that Penny half expected Kitty to comment on it but, to her surprise, she didn't.

"I'm so glad," Kitty said, "that nothing was stolen." She too, wore black tonight, a strapless bodice with a clinging skirt and a short train. From her ears hung rubies that were spectacular.

"Nothing at all is missing," Don said blandly. "It's too bad you and Mrs. Owens were disturbed."

"Oh, I adore excitement," Kitty assured him with a brittle laugh and again Penny saw her mother give her that troubled look.

It seemed to her that they had never sat so long at the table, that the long summer twilight was fading faster than ever before. It would soon be very dark. What should she do? She realized that, imperative as it was for her to meet the draftsman without fail, she should not go off on such an errand without telling someone what she was doing. Someone on whose loyalty she could rely.

Don would not let her go. He would keep the appointment himself. She knew him well enough for that. A suspicious move on his part would not only endanger him but would endanger the man who was risking his life to warn them. No, she could not tell Don.

She watched Fane as he moved around the table. He was cool and as assuredly the perfect servant as ever. Why did he always turn up behind her when she met the draftsman? Accident? Coincidence? Why was he watching her every move? Or was he watching Petro? Was it Fane who had terrified him so much that day he had hidden at the garage? It was maddening not to know.

Had Fane seen her discover the note when she had unwrapped the bandage from Vag's leg? At least, he would not be able to find and read it. She had burned the scraps.

Penny's heart lurched. Fane might not have seen the draftsman's face, but suppose he remembered Vag? It would be easy to find out who the dog's owner was.

She was roused from her absorption by the sound of a laugh and looked up to find Kitty watching her. At the opposite end of the table Don too was watching her, his face anxious.

"I've been speaking and speaking to you," Kitty said. "But you've been in a brown study. I don't believe you heard a single word."

"I'm so sorry," Penny said.

"Does your head ache?" Don asked quickly.

"I—perhaps it does," Penny said. It was easier to account for her absent-mindedness that way. She got to her feet and her guests followed while Don preceded them to open the door. As she passed him she said in a low tone, "Will you make my excuses, Don, and entertain our guests this evening? I think I'll—go up to my room."

"The best thing you could do," he agreed promptly. "I'll send Nora to you."

"No," Penny said quickly. Too quickly, she wondered? She did not want to arouse suspicion. "Nora had so little sleep last night and I won't need her." Not where I am going, she added to herself.

Don lifted her hand to his lips. "Rest all you can," he said tenderly.

"Turtledoves," Kitty Scarlet remarked and Don let Penny's hand go, though his eyes followed her up the stairs.

In her room she quickly changed from high-heeled shoes to moccasins, removed the Chinese-red jacket and pulled on a black cardigan that would blend with the night and conceal her gleaming arms and throat. She scrawled a brief note: *Geoff, I am going to meet a man who knows about the danger to Don. If I am not back in an hour, you'd better take action. Otherwise, don't mention this to anyone. I'll be careful.* She added, as a gay note of assurance, *Lucky Penny.*

She tapped lightly at Geoff's door. It was opened by Macy. She could see Geoff sitting on his balcony with his dinner table in front of him. Because she dared not stop for explanations, for fear Geoff would prevent her from going, she did not call out to him and he did not see her.

She handed the note to the valet. "Will you give this to Mr. Jarvis?"

Macy bowed as he took it, glanced in surprise at the black cardigan, at the moccasins on her feet. The door closed. For a moment Penny was uneasy. She felt that she had blundered in letting the man observe the changes in her costume. It would be obvious to him that she was planning to leave the house. But it was too late now. She must get away before Geoff read the note and stopped her.

117

She went noiselessly down the stairs. Listened. She heard Don's voice, Kitty's laugh, a comment from Mrs. Owens. They were having coffee in the morning room instead of in the drawing room. That made it awkward, as the morning room faced on the garden through which she wanted to leave the estate. For a moment, Penny hesitated. To go out the front door, down the driveway, along the main highroad was too risky.

She paused and then opened Don's study door and went into the room. Only one light had been turned on, the one that illuminated the portrait of Don's father. The strong fine face glowed in the darkened room. Penny stood looking at it earnestly. That was how Don would look in twenty years. Don! Nothing must happen to him.

She started to put her hand on the light switch and then withdrew it. To turn on the light might do more harm than good. Someone might notice it, come to find out who had turned it. And yet she longed for the comfort and reassurance of light. She hated the thought of the darkness into which she had to go.

She took a long breath, moved noiselessly toward the open French windows, wondering as she did why they had been left open at a time when Uplands was practically in a state of siege. She stepped out on the gravel path and for an instant the path of light streaming from the morning room windows touched her face. She dodged quickly into the shadows of the hedge and began to run.

In the morning room, Don was apologizing for Penny's absence. She had a severe headache, he said, and he had thought it best for her to go to bed.

"I thought she didn't look well," Kitty said. "I have barely caught a glimpse of her all day."

"She stayed in bed to rest."

"Not all the time," Kitty said in surprise. "Dick Wentworth called to see her this afternoon."

"I'm sure she didn't receive him."

"Oh, she did," Kitty said. "They had quite a talk in the garden."

Don got up, walked to the window, looked out. Kitty joined him. "Dick is a very persistent man," she said.

"My wife is not interested in Wentworth," Don said coldly. "Whatever impression he may have attempted to give you. I know Penny too well to believe——" His voice broke off, died in his throat.

There was a footstep on gravel, a shadow moved through

the open study doors, stood for a moment in the light from
the morning room. Don saw the upturned face. Penny! Then
she darted into the shadows, out of sight. He heard her running.

XVIII

Out of sight of the house Penny came to a halt. The
darkness of the night closed around her like a tangible thing.
It seemed to her that she could stretch out a hand and touch
it. And the darkness threatened her. I'm afraid, she admitted
to herself. But I have to go on. She thought about the trip
ahead. By following the highway, she could reach the icehouse after about a mile's walking. By cutting through the
fields and a portion of the state forest she could reach it in
a quarter of a mile. But the forest at night was too risky. She
decided to stick to the highway.

She opened the side door of the garage and felt her way
into the tool room. On the usual shelf she found what she
was looking for, a big lantern-shaped flashlight with a handle
on top that she could slip over her wrist if she needed to keep
her hands free. She tried it, found it worked perfectly, snapped
it off. She really ought to have a weapon of some sort, she
thought, and after a second's hesitation, put back the flashlight and selected another one, long and heavy. It was not so
convenient to carry but more useful if she had to protect
herself. Like a heavy club.

She must not think of that. She slipped quietly outside, her
dress and black cardigan as dark as the night, her moccasins
noiseless on the grass, and made her way out to the drive. She
kept carefully on the grass at the side of the gravel road and
followed it down to the highway and through the big gates.

Uplands was behind her now. Sheltered from its upper
windows by the mammoth hedge that shut off the estate from
the road, she flashed on the light and walked quickly along
the highway.

Hours had passed since Petro had sent her his message,
since he had asked her to hurry. Suppose, in the meantime,
something had happened to him! She was so preoccupied with
the coming meeting that she was not in the least afraid. The
air of the summer night was balmy, so mild, indeed, that the
wrap was almost too warm, but she kept it on because it

concealed her bare arms. What was the danger within Uplands? And who was the person responsible? That was the thought that disturbed her most. Remembering that she was leaving Don behind, leaving him under the same roof with someone who was his enemy, she almost turned back.

But there was no point in doing that until she knew the identity of Don's enemy, until she had heard what the draftsman had to tell her. She quickened her pace. Saw the high beam of headlights over the crest of a low rise, turned off her own light and moved as far off the road as she dared. A car came over the ridge. She heard a radio tuned loud, a burst of music that faded, the car moved out of sight. She turned on her flashlight again.

The estates were large and far apart on this road and there was, as a rule, little traffic. After a while a truck passed, changed gear on the incline, went over the hill and disappeared.

How quiet it was! In the woods nothing stirred, as though the woods animals, the very trees, were waiting, listening. The only sound was that of her own light steps on the road.

And then she heard a car behind her. Heard—not saw! She turned out her flashlight and looked around. A hundred yards back of her a car was turning on the winding road, creeping toward her. It was using only parking lights.

Penny stood motionless, more puzzled than alarmed. Instinct rather than reason made her glance quickly around, dart off the road and crouch behind a huge maple tree with a double trunk.

The car came on, still moving slowly. The moon was rising and casting a milky light over the landscape. An odd-shaped bush cast a strange shadow, like a hunchbacked man. The car stopped. Suddenly, blindingly, a big searchlight was turned on the bush.

Inside the car someone grunted impatiently. The light went out.

". . . I know you did," said the voice Penny had heard before. "But I was so sure it was the girl crouching there—"

"You've done it now. Might as well turn on your lights." The voice was whispering. How difficult it was to tell anything about a voice that whispered. Man or woman? Penny did not know.

The car lights came on. Penny lay with her face almost against the ground. They were hunting for her! This time there was no stolen car left on the road to help her escape, no chance of a state policeman coming to her rescue. There was no one on the road but the men who were looking for her. Even if a car should come she would not have time to hail it before they caught her, silenced her.

She pressed her trembling lips firmly together. Took a long breath. Made herself relax. At least, she comforted herself, Geoff knew where she had gone. If anything—happened to her he would start a pursuit within an hour, less than an hour. They couldn't—do anything very terrible to her in an hour. Or could they?

"Well, we've lost her," said the voice Penny knew. There was a murmur. "I picked you up five minutes after she left the house. I couldn't have done more. She came this way."

Another murmur.

"But where could she have been going? The Meredith place is the nearest and that's several miles. Part of a state park cuts in here and no private property can be sold."

The murmur.

"No, not a thing. Well, there's an old abandoned icehouse but—"

The murmur.

". . . . on the chance, yes. But it's a slim chance."

The car crept off, the lights burning, the great searchlight moving from side to side.

Penny's hand covered her mouth to smother her scream. No, no, they must not go to the icehouse! She had no way of warning Petro. He would be caught.

Well, there was still the state forest. She switched on her light and began to run over the rough ground. Her long net skirt caught on brambles and she jerked it away, regardless of tears. The car was moving so slowly, barely more than a walk, searching for her. She still had a chance.

Wild blackberry bushes whipped across her face, scratching it, and she pushed them impatiently aside. Once her flashlight reflected small twin torches and a deer turned and thrashed away among the trees. Once it revealed a cat with fur of wide black and white stripes. Penny stopped short, heart in her mouth. Better a dangerous animal than a skunk, she thought. But the skunk, too, made off without paying attention to her. For which she was devoutly thankful.

There were other nocturnal things in the woods but there was not time to think of them now. Nature was kind compared with so-called civilized man. Her danger was not in the forest; it was riding down the open highway in a modern car.

The icehouse was set back a couple of hundred feet from the road. There was no light. Penny ran toward it with a sob of relief. And then the isolated situation, the darkness, began to terrify her.

Suppose that Petro was not there? Suppose that his message, like the one purported to come from the army camp, was a fake? After all, she knew nothing about him. She and Don had witnessed his attempt to climb the trellis. The state police had warned her grimly of her danger, had ordered her not to go off anywhere by herself.

Behind her were the dark woods, ahead the dark icehouse. Who and what was inside? What awaited her?

She hesitated, almost yielding to the temptation to run back the way she had come. Then she made her choice. She called softly, "Petro, are you there? It's Mrs. Garth."

She heard a creaking sound as the rusty hinges moved complainingly. She felt rather than saw the shadowy figure that emerged. For an instant her flashlight pinned Petro against the door, a white face, eyes that seemed to glare into the light. Then she turned the flash briefly on her own face to reassure him and switched it off.

He was beside her now. "You came," he said aloud. "When I had waited so long I began to be afraid you had not found my message or that you did not trust me. I thought you would not come."

"Hush," Penny said, her voice a mere thread of sound. "You've got to get away from here at once. They'll be here any moment. By road. In a car. I was followed. That's why I took the short cut through the woods."

He did not wait for further explanation. "We'll have to hurry. I left a bundle of clothes in there. They'd know I'd been at the icehouse."

He took her flashlight, ran back to the icehouse and returned, carrying a knapsack which he flung over his shoulders. They heard the sound of a motor in the still night and he caught her hand.

"We'll have to get into the woods. Are you afraid?"

"I came that way," she reminded him.

His hand held hers. The flashlight was only an added danger to them now and he did not turn it on. His right hand grasped it as though it were a club. He led the way, walking with the catlike tread of an Indian and she followed, step by step. He stumbled into a bush, stopped, drew back, pulled her around it. He dropped flat on the ground and she followed suit, crouching beside him.

"Keep your face covered," he said, his voice muffled.

The great spotlight moved, searching through the night, found the icehouse. Stayed there. The car door slammed. Then a voice shouted, "Come out, Petro! We know you're there."

Penny could not see the man beside her, but the hand which still gripped hers was icy. She could feel the tremor in his arm.

"Turn the searchlight into the icehouse," the voice directed. The beam moved, fell on the open door. There were footsteps. Someone was walking inside, moving cautiously. Then a voice shouted, "No one here. Hasn't been anyone here that I can see."

There was a pause while the two people hidden behind the fragile protection of a wild blackberry bush waited. The man who had searched the icehouse returned to the car. Voices murmured. They waited in the night, pursuers and pursued.

Then at last the car door slammed, the motor hummed, the car moved on, the great searchlight was switched off.

Penny started to get up and the hand dragged her down. "Wait," Petro whispered urgently. "It may be a trick. They won't give up so easily."

At length he raised his head cautiously. He listened. Then he tugged at her hand. "All right. They've gone. We'd better talk while we can."

That talk in the darkness was the strangest and most poignant experience that Penny had ever had. From the hushed voice of the young man beside her, scarcely older than herself, she learned of a world that, in her sheltered life, she had not dreamed could exist.

A world in which young men and women crouched and hid like this, and took it for granted as a part of normal life. A world in which fear was a normal ingredient in the air one breathed. But a world where, in spite of that accustomed fear, they were hoping, working, risking all they had—their lives —to break the spell of fear and make the world a safe place for others, if it could not be for themselves.

He pressed some folded papers into her hand. "I'm giving you the address of my brothers and sisters. If—anything happens to me—there will be no one to help them. I don't know exactly what you and Mr. Garth could do but—any-

123

how, now that I'm not trusted, the youngsters will be in danger. There may be some way to save them from retaliation."

"We'll do our best," Penny said fervently, tears running down her cheeks. "We'll do our best."

"That's all I can ask." Petro added proudly, "If they knew I'd made this choice, gambled their safety and their lives in order not to betray my new country, they would understand. They would accept that decision."

Tears stung behind Penny's eyelids.

Petro's tone changed, became brisk and impersonal. "Now then—" He told her the story of the secret plane and of the attempts to get hold of the plans. He repeated much that she had already known. Men were planted in the various departments. "One of those papers I gave you contains the names I know, but there may be others. They found it practically impossible to piece together the isolated bits of information and get what they wanted. So they opened Mr. Garth's safe at the Works. The blueprints aren't there. Then they decided to get hold of him and make him talk. I was—was supposed to take him to them."

As the girl gasped, he said, "I know how it sounds. But at least I didn't do it. Then, when they began to distrust me, they tried to get you, so Mr. Garth would have to come to them with ransom money and would fall into their hands. I—tried to warn him but something went wrong. He didn't get my message or didn't understand it."

Petro's knees sagged. Penny tried to steady him.

"Are you hurt?" she asked.

He laughed softly. "Just faint from hunger."

She gave a little exclamation of horror. Stifled it. A car was coming—which direction? Coming slowly. It was the car that had followed her. Returning. Again it was crawling along, the searchlight sweeping every foot of the highway from side to side, sending long fingers of light reaching out into the woods.

Petro dragged Penny down on the ground and they waited. It seemed hours, but it was probably only a matter of seconds, before the car had passed.

He tried to get up but he was too weak. "You've got to get away," he told her desperately, "and I'm not strong enough to go with you."

"I won't leave you," Penny declared.

"You must," he said firmly. "Listen, this is what I want you to tell Mr. Garth. They believe the blueprints must be at Uplands, in Mr. Garth's safe there. They are going to raid the place in force and get them. This time they are risking everything and they won't be stopped. Not by anything. Not by anybody. They are desperate. They have to show some real results at once to make up for that blundering kidnaping attempt."

Penny was silent, thinking quickly.

"You'll need all the help you can get. You've got to set a trap at Uplands. And Mr. Garth must be kept out of danger." Petro added imploringly, "Please go. Hurry!"

"They can't get in the house," Penny said to reassure him.

"They'll be admitted by——" His voice stopped. He fell forward.

"Petro," she whispered. "Petro."

She bent over. Touched his face. He had fainted. She rubbed his wrists. He stirred. "Brandy," he whispered. "Left it in the icehouse. Take the flashlight."

He thrust it into her hand and she switched it on, ran to the icehouse, went inside. She moved the light from side to side. The place was empty. There was nothing there. She ran back. The knapsack lay where Petro had left it. He was gone.

"Petro," she called softly, not daring to lift her voice. "Petro! I know you haven't gone far. You're hiding. Waiting for me to go alone because you think I'll have a better chance. Petro! Please answer me."

There was no sound.

Penny choked back a sob. Somewhere in the darkness he was hiding, weak and exhausted, so that she could escape. This was his choice.

"All right," she said aloud. "I'll hurry. I'll do the best I can. Thank you, Petro. And God bless you."

She switched on the light and began to retrace her steps through the darkness and the undergrowth of the state forest. The forest seemed to come alive. It was not still as it had been before. Animals moved restlessly, the trees rustled like whispering voices. Brambles caught at her like clutching fingers.

I can't go on, she thought. I'm afraid. I'm afraid. She turned off the flashlight when she came to a clearing for fear it would be seen by watching eyes on the highway. Lifted her head. Through the open space there was nothing but darkness, and then, above her was a single bright star, like a beckoning hand, like a message. She looked at it, nodded her head as though in answer, and went on into the woods.

Curious how fear had left her. She moved swiftly and surely now, thinking only of the warning she must take to Don, conscious only of her goal.

At length she felt smooth grass under her feet. She had reached Uplands! She went quickly across the lawn, let herself in through the study windows and made her way on tiptoe to her room. She slipped inside and closed her door. Leaned against it, exhausted. And somewhere, like an echo, she heard another door close softly.

XIX

Whose door had closed? Who had seen her creep up the stairs to her room? Penny leaned against her door for support. The only people on the second floor were Don, Geoff, Kitty Scarlet and Mrs. Owens. Geoff could not move around his room with that broken leg. Mrs. Owens went to bed at ten-thirty and slept soundly. Don or Kitty, then. But why, why would either of them spy on her? Anyone seeing her must know that she had had an accident, would want to help. Wouldn't they?

Penny locked her door, feeling odd as she did so. Never in her life had she locked a door in a private house. Whom would you lock out in a dwelling filled with people you trusted? Then she switched on the light, looked carefully around the small sitting room, went into her bedroom and turned on the lights there, switched on the lights in the bathroom. Feeling half ashamed of herself, she peeked behind the shower curtains, looked in the closets, under the bed. Then at last she drew an unsteady breath of relief. No one there. No one hidden.

She caught sight of herself in the mirror and gasped. Was that Penelope Garth? The moccasins were caked with mud to which bits of leaves and twigs were sticking. The black net skirt hung in great jagged tears that dragged on the carpet. Her hair was disheveled, a couple of leaves sticking to it where she had lain with her face pressed against the ground. And her face—it was filthy.

She took off her clothes, bathed, using lots of bath salts, reached for a robe and changed her mind. There were things to do before the night was over. A glance at her tiny jeweled wristwatch told her that it was after midnight. She put on a brown tailored skirt, an emerald-green sweater, brushed and tied back her hair with a brown ribbon, found low walking shoes. Now she was equipped for anything.

For anything, yes. But what should she do first? She sat down on a low slipper chair in her bedroom, hands clasped around her knees, eyes on the sturdy brown shoes, and tried to make herself think clearly. She had not really thought all evening. Things had happened too fast, there had been too much panic in the air.

Since she had found herself back at Uplands her head had been behaving queerly. She was dizzy, she had a curious sense of unreality. There was something that she must do, must do at once. If she could only remember it! Why was she wearing brown walking shoes at this time of night? Why not evening slip—of course, she had just changed them. But why? She'd been out—she'd—Petro!

What was wrong with her, wrong with her head, that she'd forgotten young Petro, who was being tracked down, who had offered himself as a sacrifice to save Don, who had disappeared into the woods so that she would have a better chance to escape?

He was weak, hungry, frightened. He was alone. And his enemies would never give up. Penny began to shiver. Somewhere, now, this very minute, Petro was alone in the night, waiting for the men to come back, to find him. Somewhere, now, this very minute, the car was creeping along the road, the spotlight reaching out hungry fingers of light into the woods, prodding the underbrush, seeking out a man.

A sob rose in her throat. We must find Petro before the others do. We've got to protect him. But she did not move. She did not seem able to move. And then, through the swirling mists in her mind she heard Petro crying urgently, "Hurry! Hurry!"

Of course. The concussion or shock was making her behave very oddly, making her forget. They must set a trap at Uplands. The men were coming here. If she could only remember what she was supposed to do. Hurry, she told herself, and walked slowly toward the door like a person walking through deep water. It was a tremendous effort to walk but she had to keep going. Before she forgot again how important it was.

She paused for a moment in her sitting room, reluctant to unlock the door, to step out into the hall. Ridiculous, she told herself sharply. Aren't you ashamed of yourself, Penny? What could possibly happen to you at Uplands? And then she remembered the knowledge that had hovered on the brink of her mind, that the core of the danger lay at Uplands and that Petro had not been able to tell her who was responsible.

Which one? she thought. Which one?

And now, like a door opening slowly, letting light into a dark room, her mind began to clear. Hours had passed, two hours and a half to be exact, since she had left the house to keep her appointment with Petro at the abandoned icehouse. And Geoff had not sent help. What did that mean?

With swift decision she unlocked the door and went out into the corridor. The house was still. She tapped softly at the door of Don's bedroom which was next to her own. It opened instantly as though he had been waiting. He wore a brocaded dressing gown. He had not gone to bed. The room was dim with smoke. He must have been walking the floor and smoking for hours.

His eyes flicked over her face, noticed her change of costume. They were a stranger's eyes, as cold as ice. He waited politely for her to speak.

"Don," she said, a catch in her voice, "don't look at me like that. As though we were strangers."

"We are strangers, Penelope." Was that his voice? It couldn't be.

"What's the matter?" she demanded.

He laughed harshly. "You know the answer to that better than I do. The funny thing is that I really believed that I could trust you."

"But—"

"And then you sneak off after dinner to meet Dick Wentworth."

"I—what?—Dick—" Penny was so astounded that the words sputtered from her lips like a boiling teakettle. Then as the meaning of what he had said was impressed on her she became cold and white with anger. "Don," she exclaimed, head high, eyes blazing. "I would never have believed you could insult me so."

She turned away from his door, leaving him standing there. She went to Geoff's room and knocked. Knocked a second time. A sleepy voice asked, "What is it?"

"Geoff, it's Penny."

"Come in," he said in a startled tone. She opened the door. Geoff reached for the light beside his bed and turned it on. "What's wrong, Penny?"

She looked at him with equal surprise. "What's the matter with everyone?" she exclaimed. "You just—went to sleep?"

He blinked at her. "Why shouldn't I?" he said mildly.

"If that is the way you are trying to protect Don, no wonder—"

She whirled around to go out when he said sharply, "What's this all about?"

"I thought," she began hotly, "that when you got my note, you'd at least wait to go to sleep until you found out whether I'd returned safely."

"What note?"

"The one I gave Macy."

"Wait a minute, gal," Geoff said. "When was this? I never got a note. What do you mean about getting back safely?"

"Macy—didn't give it to you?"

Geoff shook his head. He reached toward the bell. "Wait, Geoff! Don't call him. Something is terribly wrong. Macy—" For a moment she was wide-eyed. Incredulous. "Geoff, I should have known! It was Macy's voice. The voice in the car. The man who kidnaped me. It was Macy tonight!"

"If you don't tell me what this is all about, Penelope Garth, I'll go right out of my mind," Geoff said desperately. "One of us is stark, staring crazy."

Penny told him then about the note she had received from Petro, about leaving a message with Macy, saying she had gone to meet the draftsman and that if she did not return in an hour Geoff was to take action.

"Penny!" he said, appalled. "You mean you went out alone after what had happened to you? What in heaven's name possessed you to take a chance like that? If I'd known what you were up to, I'd have come after you, cast and all."

"You'd have followed my wife—where?" Don asked in frosty accents from the doorway.

"Don't be a fool," Geoff said promptly. "Come in here, Don, and shut the door. We've got to have a council of war and maybe you can hammer some sense into the head of this chance-taking wife of yours."

Don and Penny did not look at each other. Don came inside and shut the door, leaned against it, waited.

"Now then, Penny," Geoff directed. "Start at the beginning."

"All right." She drew an uneven breath and began with finding the dog Vag, of its owner, Petro, following her home, of his saying he would thank her in actions rather than in deeds.

"Who is this man Petro?" Garth demanded.

"A draftsman at the Works. He's the one we saw trying to climb the trellis, the one who tried to warn you that you were in danger."

Garth gave a sharp exclamation.

Penny went on quickly. Petro had come to Uplands to get his dog and he had been terrified, he had hidden around the side of the garage. Someone at the house had scared him, someone he recognized and wanted to avoid.

"Who was it?" Geoff asked.

"I thought all the time," Penny said, "that it was Fane. He was right behind me when I was speaking to Petro. In fact, it seems to me that wherever I go, Fane is right there, listening."

"Fane," Garth said thoughtfully, remembering the butler's interest in his comings and goings, his report by telephone on the time he left the house. He started toward the door. "We'll clear this up right now."

"No, Don, no!" Penny exclaimed. "Not yet. I've got a lot more to tell you. I think now the one who frightened him was Macy.—No, don't go yet. I've got something important to say."

She told him about Petro sending the dog to her with the message. For a moment she hesitated. She did not want to tell Don that Vag had driven away Dick Wentworth when he tried to make love to her. After Garth's inexcusable accusation of a few minutes before she did not want any further mention of Dick's name. Already, it had destroyed the love she had begun to feel for him. He had no faith in her if he could believe so ugly a thing simply because Kitty had told him it was true.

She explained that she had given Macy a note for Geoff— "Which," Geoff broke in, "Macy never gave me"—and slipped out of the house to meet the draftsman.

"Why didn't you tell me?" Don asked. His face whitened as he thought of the chance she had taken.

"Because," Penny said simply, "he was risking his life to warn you. It was better to protect him if I possibly could. I owed him that for what he was doing for you."

"Penny!"

She ignored the tortured cry of apology in his voice. She described her trip to the icehouse and the car that had crept along the road, seeking her.

The two men listened breathlessly, picturing that pursuit in the dark, the girl alone and unarmed, suffering from concussion; the ruthless trackers following her.

"One of them," she interrupted her story, speaking to Geoff rather than to Don, "was Macy. I know that now. He

130

saw my moccasins and black cardigan when I came to your door to leave the note. How could I have been so dumb? I might as well have worn a placard announcing that I was going out."

"But I don't understand," Geoff said, perplexed, "how he dared hold back the note. He must have known that sooner or later you would tell me about it."

"I don't think," Penny said quietly, "he expected that I would return."

Geoff bit his lip hard and Don took out a handkerchief with a shaking hand and wiped his face.

Quickly she reported her meeting with Petro, the ghastly game of hide-and-seek they had played in the woods with the searchlight from the car. She told how Petro had been too weak to escape and had tricked her into going back by herself so she'd have a better chance, unburdened by him.

"Penny!" Regardless of Geoff's presence, Don swept her into his arms, his eyes blazing, face white. "Penny, my brave, loyal darling! Forgive me. Please forgive me. But I was mad with jealousy and Kitty told me you'd seen Dick secretly this afternoon. Then we saw you slip out of the house——"

She released herself with gentle dignity and a finality that chilled Garth. "It's too late, Don," she said sadly. "If Kitty's word has more weight with you than mine——"

As he started to protest she held up her hand. "There's no time now to consider personal matters. Petro is in danger. We've got to find him at once. And there is danger in this house." The words poured out clearly now as she explained that the enemy believed the blueprints to be at Uplands, that they intended to make a last desperate effort to get them.

"We've got to have help at once," she said crisply. "And we've got to protect Petro." She handed Don the list of names Petro had given her. "These are the men—as many of them as he knows—who have been planted at the Works."

As Don looked over the list he gave an ejaculation of surprise. "Some of these men I would have trusted completely!"

"What are you going to do about Macy? I've found him in your study once before."

"I don't believe he will come back here," Geoff said.

"But he doesn't know that I got back safely," Penny pointed out. "He must be the one who was to admit the others."

Geoff groaned. "If only I could walk! I can't stay penned up here while things are happening. Out of all the action."

131

"Geoff," Don asked, "have you a revolver?"

Geoff leaned over and took a heavy automatic out of the drawer of the bedside table.

"Loaded?"

He nodded grimly. He didn't, Penny thought, look much like a playboy at this moment.

"Penny," Don directed, "you stay here where Geoff can guard you until I get back."

He left the room, closing the door behind him. They heard his voice in the hall. He sounded startled. "Kitty! Anything the matter?"

"No," Kitty said in her high sweet voice, "but I heard people talking and I was afraid Geoff was in pain." Before Don could stop her, she had opened the door and stood looking in. The violet eyes were a trifle fixed as they rested on the businesslike-looking revolver lying beside Geoff's hand.

Her eyes traveled slowly to Penny, looked at the sweater and skirt, the low walking shoes. Although hours had passed since she had withdrawn to her own room and presumably gone to bed, she still was in evening dress.

She did not seem to notice that no one spoke, that no one asked her to come in. She walked forward and sat down coolly. "My dear," she said sweetly to Penny, "do you think you ought to spend so much time with Geoff, unchaperoned?"

Penny was too furious to reply. It was Geoff who exclaimed, "Kitty, I didn't know you could be so malicious. It isn't like you."

Delicate color swept over Kitty's face. Her lips tightened. Then she smiled faintly. "How'd you leave Dick tonight?" she asked Penny.

"Dick!" This was the second time she had been accused of seeing Dick Wentworth that night. "I haven't seen him."

"But, my dear," Kitty protested. "I saw you myself."

Don came back into the room in dark slacks and a navy-blue sport shirt, rubber-soled shoes on his feet. "All right," he said quickly. "Everything is organized. Uplands can stand a real siege at this point. Kitty, will you please go to your room and lock the door? Have your mother do the same thing. Neither of you will be in any danger if you obey orders."

The young widow looked at him for a long moment with an indefinable smile around her red lips. Then she nodded. "Whatever you say, Don," she agreed sweetly, "though I might point out that I am not in the least afraid of danger. In fact, it rather—thrills me." She went out without another word.

Don held the door for Penny. "Will you go to your room, please?"

"But what are you going to do about Petro?"

"First, we've got to protect the blueprints and round up this gang," he said.

"But a man's life is at stake, Don!" she cried in protest. "How can you be so—"

"So woodeny?" he asked with a short laugh. "More than one man's fate is at stake, Penelope. The bigger issue must take precedence. We'll do everything we can for the man. But later."

She did not move, watching him from long-lashed eyes, a puzzled look that stirred his heart. He longed to take her in his arms. Instead, he said matter-of-factly, "Now I want you to go to your room. And stay there."

"I'm not going to my room," she said stormily. "I won't be treated like a child."

Don smiled down at her, swept her up in his arms, carried her to her own suite, set her down inside the sitting room. Before she could prevent it, he had reached for the key. He closed the door and she heard the key turn in the lock from the outside.

XX

Locked in! Tonight she had risked her life to help Donald Garth and he believed that she had sneaked away—sneaked! —from his house to see Dick Wentworth. Now he had locked her in her room, probably to prevent her from going out to have a second meeting.

Penny was shocked at the extent of her own cold anger. Cold? It was flaming hot. To distrust her! To lock her up like a—like a naughty child. Or worse, like a criminal.

Through the heavy door and the walls that deadened sound in the superbly built house she could hear muffled activity, muted voices, hushed movements of people. All of Uplands seemed to be stirring. They were prepared, Don said, for a siege. At least, poor Petro had achieved his purpose. His warning had got through. Don was ready for anything that might come.

Petro! He was the one who was not prepared. Weak from hunger, faint from exhaustion, he was hiding in the woods somewhere unless they—unless they—face it, Penny!—unless they had already found him.

Penny twisted the doorknob and in sudden fury banged on the door. Outside she heard the ghost of a laugh. Kitty was there, enjoying her imprisonment, amused by her helplessness. It was that laugh which decided Penny. She went swiftly into her bedroom. The key was gone from the door that opened into Don's room. He was taking no chances on her escape.

I'll show him he can't keep me prisoner, she decided. She stepped out on the balcony, looked down.

To her surprise there was no light showing from Don's study. She leaned farther out so that she could see along the house. There were no lights anywhere! Evidently, Don was setting his trap for Petro's former associates when they came.

Things like that can't happen at Uplands, she thought. A peaceful country house where for generations people have lived graciously, with dignity, and with trust in their fellows. They don't wait in the dark to be besieged like a medieval fortress. Yes, she remembered, they must do so when medieval forces are let loose on the world.

She took a long breath, bent over and groped until her hands closed over a stout vine. Then she climbed out on the balcony railing, eased her weight onto the vine. For a moment she hung there in the dark, swaying, aware of the frail support swaying under her. Then, slowly, feeling her way from one foothold to another, she climbed down the vine until she stood in the garden looking up at her darkened room.

Even if there were watchers in the garden, and the thought made her shiver, no one could have seen her climb down the vine, no one could have heard her.

She stole around the house to the kitchen wing. There was a crack of light. She stood on tiptoe, peered under the shade that had not been quite drawn. Nora was bustling about, making coffee, putting up sandwiches. Somewhere, there was a faint tinkle of a bell. The maid looked up at the indicator board on the wall to see from which room the bell had rung. Then she went out of the kitchen.

The window was open because of the warm night and Penny pulled herself up, got into the kitchen, filled a thermos with coffee, wrapped sandwiches in waxed paper and pushed them into a big patch pocket on her skirt. In the pantry she found a flashlight and she let herself out the back door.

She took the short cut through the woods, using the flashlight as little as possible, pausing every few yards to listen intently. There was no sound but that of the woods animals, which had so alarmed her on her first trip, and which now seemed friendly, almost reassuring.

Once she stumbled over the upthrust root of a fallen tree and nearly lost the precious thermos of coffee. Once, as she came to a clearing, she could see the highway like a broad ribbon in the moonlight. But this time nothing moved along it.

She was near the icehouse now. She had returned here almost by instinct. It had occurred to her that, after finding it empty, they would let it alone. It would be the safest place for Petro to hide.

Was he there or was he a prisoner? A muffled gleam of the flashlight. She saw the dark building, the gaping door that opened on blackness. She crept closer. This time her heart began to pound. Suppose they were waiting? Or suppose a tramp had picked out this shelter for the night. Suppose—

She stepped on a dry twig and it snapped as loudly as a revolver shot, she thought. And from inside the icehouse came a startled gasp. Then silence.

She had to make up her mind. Someone was hidden there. But who? She shifted the thermos of coffee to her left hand, gripped the flashlight so that she could use it as a defensive weapon.

"Petro," she whispered. Something stirred inside the icehouse. "Petro, it's Mrs. Garth."

He loomed up beside her so quickly that she stifled a gasp.

"Mrs. Garth!" He was thunderstruck. "I thought—I hoped you had got away."

"I did. Then I thought this would be the safest place for you because they had already searched it. I brought you some sandwiches and hot coffee."

"Bless you!" he said fervently.

They sat side by side, Turkish fashion, on the dirt floor of the icehouse while he drank the hot coffee and ate ravenously. Penny talked in whispers, telling him how she had got the message to Don, that Uplands was now ready to withstand any assault from the enemy and that she had been afraid for him. So she had come back, bringing food.

When at last he had drained the thermos and eaten every crumb of the sandwiches, he spoke to her. "Now I have strength for anything. But I hate to have you go back alone. They may be between us and Uplands, you know."

"I'm not going back alone," Penny explained. "You are going with me. You'll be safe there. My—husband will make sure that you are safe. Come on."

"Safe?" he echoed in a tone of wonder. "I had forgotten there was such a word."

"Then we will teach you to remember it," Penny said.

"But," he warned her, "they are probably somewhere between us and Uplands."

"No one ever learned safety without first learning courage," Penny said with a soft laugh. She told him about her fear when she had gone back through the woods the first time, about the star that had seemed to guide her. "Here we go."

The girl and the young man slipped out of the icehouse into the darkness of the woods. Ahead there was unknown danger but they faced it with confidence, eyes shining, a smile on their lips.

ii

Don stood in the doorway to the kitchen, a revolver in his hand.

"All right, Nora. Thank you very much. Now go up to your room and lock yourself in. Don't come out until I give you permission."

Nora stood her ground. "What about Mrs. Garth?"

"She's in her room and she'll stay there," he said grimly. "I won't let her take any more chances tonight. Now hurry. They'll be here any time and I want to check our defenses."

"I'd be happier if I could stay with Penny—Mrs. Garth," Nora said stubbornly.

Don smiled and took the key to Penny's door out of his pocket. "Run along then and stay with her," he agreed.

He checked the lock on the back door and frowned when he found it had not been turned, pulled down and fastened the window. He wanted no one coming in this way. The trap was baited on the south side of the house where the French windows to his study were invitingly ajar.

He switched out the light in the kitchen and peered through the window. He could see the garage. Something moved cautiously beside it. He smiled to himself. The chauffeur was on guard.

In the darkened dining room a man cleared his throat.

"Who's that?" Don asked, startled. His thumb touched the safety catch of his revolver.

"Fane." The butler's tone had changed. It was no longer subservient. He did not add, "sir."

A thread of light shot from a pencil torch and the butler pulled out his wallet, handed it to Don, keeping the light on it.

Don looked down. "FBI!" he exclaimed.

"Yes, Mr. Garth." There was a look of faint amusement on the ex-butler's face.

"So that's why you were checking on the time I left the house."

"Right. I had a man spotted a couple of miles down the road who trailed you to work in an old truck. Just to be on the safe side." He added grimly, "What I can't forgive myself for is letting Mrs. Garth run into that ambush. I never knew about the telephone call or even that she had left the house until it was all over. They ought to demand my resignation for that."

"Any more surprises?" Don laughed. "I must say"—he held out his hand, gripped Fane's—"that you are a pleasant one tonight. You know what's up?"

"Sure. They are planning to raid the house for the blueprints. I knew that as soon as I heard you talking to the chauffeur. I suppose—I hope the blueprints aren't really here."

"They're here all right," Don said.

"Then," Fane said soberly, "I am greatly afraid, Mr. Garth, you may have been tricked. Macy has been at your safe."

Don grinned, realized that Fane could not see his expression in the dark and said reassuringly, "I have another safe."

"I've been looking around," Fane said. "Got some reinforcements. There are three FBI men, two hiding in the study and one in front of the house. I didn't place anyone in the garden because I'd like to have your friends"—he spoke the word savagely—"walk right in. We'll just leave out the welcome mat with those open doors."

"The chauffeur has been posted on guard at the garage," Don explained. "He'll hoot like an owl if he notices anyone approaching from that direction. And the state police have men covering both sides of the house." He laughed softly. "Poor Jarvis! He's nearly crazy at being left out of the excitement. Anyone else in on this?"

"Well, yes," the pseudo-butler said in an odd tone.

Before he could go on, feet raced down the stairs and Nora, wild-eyed, said, "Where's Penny? Where's Penny? She's not upstairs. Not anywhere!"

As Don leaped toward the stairs an owl hooted.

137

"All right, Mr. Garth," Fane said crisply, "this is it."

"Not a word, Nora," Don said hoarsely. "Go up to Penny's room and lock yourself in. At once."

She looked at his face and for the first time in her life obeyed without a word.

Garth followed Fane noiselessly toward the closed door of his study. His hand was on the knob when Fane stopped him by a gentle touch of his hand on Don's sleeve. They listened. Inside the study something moved.

"Not yet," said Fane's voice so close to Don's ear that the latter could feel the FBI man's breath on his cheek. The government man was calm, unhurried. "Don't rush things or our birds will get away. The light will go on when the fellows planted in there are sure they are all in the net. We don't want the big ones to get away. Then we'll close in. But if we give the alarm now, we'll lose them."

"Do we just wait?" Don muttered.

"I'll stay here. You go out by the drawing room window and warn the man on that side that the party has begun. Then, if you can do it quietly, and I mean quietly, work your way around into the garden. But they may have a guard posted, so watch your step."

Fane pressed his ear against the study door, listening. Don crept along the hall, into the drawing room. Only one window had been left open. He looked out but a cloud had covered the moon. It was too dark to see anything.

Penny, he thought. What has happened to Penny? Has she been kidnaped again? If I have to make the choice—Penny's safety or giving the enemy the plans—no, no! A man can't be asked to make a choice like that: his country's welfare or the life of the girl he loves.

Where was she? Where was she? And Garth knew, suddenly, that he had made the bitter choice. He had put his country's welfare ahead of his personal happiness. Otherwise he would be out in the night seeking her instead of waiting to capture his enemies and those of the land he loved.

Oh, Penny, he groaned, would you forgive me if you knew? Would you understand?

His lips pressed into a thin line, his jaw hardened. Carefully, noiselessly, he eased up the screen. He put one leg over the window sill and let himself drop lightly into a flower bed below where the soft ground deadened the sound of his fall. He waited in a crouching position until his eyes adjusted to the darkness and saw the shadow that did not move. He

138

crawled forward, the shadow turned alertly, he identified himself in a whisper.

"I'm Garth. The owl hooted," he murmured. "They're getting into the study."

The shadow moved away, joined another shadow, there was a murmur of sound. The second shadow remained where it was but the first one gestured and then bent over at a stooping position so his head would not be visible. Following the gesture Don moved forward, crawling on all fours to join him, and the two men, bending low, peered around the corner of the house into the garden.

How strong the fragrance of the flowers was, Don thought idly. But that sophisticated perfume came from no flower in the garden. It was—

A faint light gleamed in the study, moved in a half circle as though signaling. Three shadows darted from the garden and through the study windows.

And then the lights came on in the study. There was a shout, scuffling, and a shot rang out.

iii

A cloud drifted over the moon and the woods were completely black. Petro's hand reached for Penny, closed around her arm. The trees stirred into life, the leaves beginning a sudden noisy chatter as the wind stirred them. The air which had been so warm had a sharp chill in it and Penny shivered.

Petro spoke in a low tone but the sound of his voice, even so muted, startled Penny who said, "Shush!"

"It's all right," he said, again speaking low. "I have been listening all the time. I am positive there is no one but us in the woods. I think they must have gone by car. It would be more logical. They aren't woodsmen. And the car provides a safe and quick getaway. Only this time," and his fingers tightened on her arm until he hurt her, "this time," he said between set teeth, "I hope they won't get away."

He was moving forward with more confidence now, using her flashlight, over which he had tied a handkerchief, to give a faint gleam of light to guide them through the undergrowth.

"Even a small light is terribly obvious in the dark," he said. "If you've been in a blackout you know how far a lighted match can be seen."

He felt her shaking. "Afraid?" he asked.

To his amazement he realized that she was shaking with laughter.

"This is my fourth trip through these woods tonight," she said. "I was just wondering what the doctor will think of my way of treating a concussion."

He stopped so abruptly that she stumbled against him. "What is it?" she asked.

His hand on her arm warned her. She peered into the darkness. Took a step forward. She was on the smooth lawn at Uplands! The house was dark. There was no sound of movement. Perhaps, after all, they weren't coming. It seemed impossible that Don was prepared, as he had said. The house seemed to be asleep.

What time was it? She tried to read her watch but she could not even see her own hand. What ghastly quiet! Even the usual noises of the night seemed to have ceased. Nature was listening too.

This suspense was unbearable. And then there was a whirr, the big clock on the landing at Uplands cleared its throat and bonged twice. Two o'clock!

Something moved! Coming along the driveway, passing the garage. An owl hooted. A flashlight gleamed, rose in a half arc of light and she felt rather than heard three people pass her, so closely that she could almost touch them. They broke into a run, their feet thudding across the grass, and entered the study.

In the quiet night air the smell of perfume was wafted to Penny. Perfume from where? Perfume close at hand where someone waited, silent in the night.

Then the lights in the study flashed on, blinding against the darkness, there were shouts, and the sound of men fighting. A shot rang out.

A man screamed a warning. Someone ran across the study, tore across the lawn.

"He's getting away," Penny sobbed in her excitement. "He's getting away."

Then a flashlight flared, pinned the man against the night and Penny cried out in shock and horror.

"Oh, no! No! No! Not Dick Wentworth!"

The sound of her voice checked the fleeing man for a moment. Before he could move. Kitty Scarlet spoke from behind the flashlight. "I warn you, Dick, not to move a step. I have you covered. I am a dead shot."

She stepped out into the light that now poured onto the lawn, still in her black evening dress, a dark scarf covering

140

her bright hair and her bare arms and shoulders, a revolver steady in her small hand.

From behind her lunged two men who seized Dick Wentworth.

XXI

"Let him go!" The words came in a snarl and the two men holding Dick Wentworth stopped short as Macy appeared before them, a revolver in his hand. But the revolver was turned, incredibly, on Penny herself. "Let him go or I'll kill the girl! Quick!"

The FBI men stood uncertainly. They were both armed but before they would be able to shoot, Macy would have time to pull the trigger.

This can't be happening to me, Penny thought. It can't. But there was death in Macy's wild eyes. He meant it. No one moved.

What happened was so completely unexpected that it took everyone off guard. Petro, standing beside Penny, suddenly knocked her down, pushing her out of range of Macy's revolver. At the same moment he dived forward, low.

Macy's revolver barked once in the night and Petro fell, twitched, lay still. Then there was another revolver shot. Lying where Petro had thrown her, Penny heard a low growl, a scuffle, and then Don's voice rang out, "I've got him, Kitty! Perfect shooting."

Penny sat up dizzily, saw Don wrest Macy's gun from him. The valet seemed to be hurt, he had fallen on the lawn. He began to scream.

Men were swarming around the house now, taking charge of the prisoners. Aside from Dick Wentworth there were two men whom Penny had never seen before. Fane—could that be Fane? she wondered in bewilderment—bent over Macy.

"Got his kneecap," he said in a calm tone. "Very nice work, Mrs. Scarlet." He beckoned to the chauffeur. "We'll need an ambulance for this bird."

Penny got shakily to her feet. Kitty Scarlet, looking as helpless as a butterfly in her trailing evening dress, held a smoking revolver in her hand. Somehow her face was not frivolous at all, her violet eyes were cool and direct.

141

"You know me?" she asked Fane in surprise.

"You were pointed out to me in London when I was consulting with my opposite number there. You were sitting in the royal box at Ascot." There was a twinkle in his eyes. "Flirting with a famous duke and looking as though you'd melt in the rain. He told me you were one of the most valuable people in his department. Sharp as a whip. No nerves. A crack shot. You've proved all that tonight."

"Petro!" Penny cried and dropped on her knees beside the unconscious man. In a moment Don reached her.

"Penny, Penny, my beloved. Are you all right?"

"Yes, but he—" her voice was unsteady. "Is he dead?"

Don knelt beside her. He turned the big light on the white-faced boy. Felt his pulse. Touched his face. "No," he said gently. "Macy's shot went through his shoulder. See? I don't think the lung is injured. He fainted, that's all." He called, "We need a doctor here and we need him fast."

He got up, helped Penny to her feet, his arm around her. She released herself quietly and turned to Dick, still standing between his captors. He looked back at her, defiantly. She did not speak but the tears ran down her cheeks. The tears did more to him than open recrimination or bitter words. His face whitened.

"You, Dick!" she said brokenly, brushing her hand over her wet eyes. "You! A traitor to your country! A criminal!" She cried out, "How could you? Oh, how could you?"

He stood at bay, an FBI man at either side, looking at the wreckage of his bright dreams of power and easy money.

"It's easy for you to talk," he exploded wrathfully. "You've got what you wanted. All you had to do was to marry a rich man. Kitty is filthy with money. Garth was born with a silver spoon in his mouth. But I had nothing. Do you suppose I'd have done this if I had had enough money?"

One of his companions in the background, who was handcuffed, snarled, "Was that it—money? Not for the cause?"

Dick gave a mirthless laugh. "The cause? No, why should I? It just offered me money. Why should I care who pays it? I need money, I tell you. I couldn't even afford to keep Macy."

He looked down at the man who was still writhing and moaning in pain. Macy lifted his head. A ferret, Penny had said, but a loyal ferret. He looked at Wentworth with doglike devotion.

"You never lost me sir," he said. "I got the job with Garth as you told me to. I kept an eye on him and watched your interests. I helped you get in tonight. I helped you kidnap the girl. I'd have shot her to help you get away——"

"Shut up," Wentworth yelled at him. "Stop talking. You're talking too much, you fool."

Macy winced as though Wentworth had struck him.

Wentworth turned to Penny. "I really loved you. If you'd just been reasonable, agreed to divorce Garth and ask for alimony. With his money——"

She turned her back.

"I wouldn't have hurt him," he stuttered, seeing Garth's expression. "When I came to see you this afternoon——"

"You came to find out whether she had recognized you, whether she guessed you had been one of the kidnapers," Kitty intervened. "You gave yourself away when you said you'd come to see how she was. There was not a word of publicity about Mrs. Garth's accident."

There was a clanging bell and an ambulance stopped in the driveway. White-coated men came out on the terrace, men so accustomed to violence that they merely raised their brows at the sight of the two men sprawled on the lawn. They laid Macy on a stretcher, then bent over Petro.

"This man stays at Uplands," Don said. "We'll see that he gets every attention here. He saved my wife's life tonight."

There was a brief scuffle. Wentworth wrenched away from the men who had been holding his arms, bent over the unconscious Petro.

"That's the man I got into the country, got him his job. And he double-crossed me." He drew back his foot to kick and Don reached him before the others could stir, his fist moved in an arc. Dick fell, a surprised look on his handsome face.

"Take him away," Don said in disgust.

There was a general movement toward the cars that had gathered in the driveway. One of the men jerked Dick to his feet. Only then did he realize clearly that he was caught, that the game was up.

His eyes moved, in craven fear, from face to face, seeking for help, for pity. "Penny," he cried. "Penny, don't let them take me! Don't let them——" His cries came back to them as he stumbled away, propelled by the hands on either arm.

ii

Penny covered her ears with her hands to shut out his

143

frightened appeals for help and ran across the lawn, into the deserted study. The place was a shambles. Glass in the French doors had been shattered. It was strewn all over the thick carpet. The draperies hung crookedly from their rods. The room looked as though a cyclone had swept through it. The safe door was wide-open. Two chairs kicked heels in the air. Desk drawers lay upside down on the carpet with papers flung about.

Penelope sank into the heavy ornate desk chair and dropped her head on her outstretched arms on the desk. She was not thinking. So much had happened that she could not think. Her mind seemed to be churned by a giant egg beater. Petro lying unconscious with blood seeping from a hole in his shoulder; Kitty holding a revolver in her hand; Dick, white-faced and terrified, as they dragged him away to the punishment he so richly deserved; Macy, doglike in his fidelity to an unworthy master, threatening to kill her; Fane—Fane an FBI man!

Nothing was the way she had thought it was. Nobody. Her head rocked. She felt cold. Icy cold. Now that it was all over, she began to shake. The pain in her head was almost beyond enduring. The effects of the kidnaping, the concussion, shock, her trips through the woods, the intolerable excitement of the last hour had caught up with her, taken their toll.

The most overwhelming fact was the one clearest in her mind. "Oh, how could Dick—" She was not conscious that she had spoken the words aloud until a voice answered her.

"A man in desperate need of funds, and without the character to work for them, will do much for money."

With a startled cry the girl looked up into Kitty Scarlet's eyes. The woman's face was white and she seemed to have aged. It was as though she had dropped the mask of vivacity and frivolity and the real woman, disillusioned, heart-weary, worldly-wise, stood revealed.

With a murmur of sympathetic understanding, Penny rose to her feet. "Do sit down," she said gently, "you must be exhausted by all this."

"No, thank you. If I were to relax I would lose my nerve, I think." Kitty smiled. "For some reason the zest for excitement no longer carries me through scenes of violence. I could never endure hearing a man scream with agony. Even if he is evil, even if he is dangerous. I am tired, I think, in my very soul."

Her radiant smile appeared as she attempted to shake off her mood. "You are the one who needs rest. But the time has come to explain to you why I asked to be invited to Uplands, why I forced myself upon you and Don during your honeymoon. And, particularly, why I got Dick Wentworth to come to this house. I am profoundly sorry that was necessary. I did not know at the time about your—previous attachment to him or that Don was jealous. Though," she admitted candidly, "it would not have mattered. What was at stake was more important than any individual happiness. I don't suppose you can understand that."

"Yes," Penny said quietly, "I can understand that now. A few hours ago, certainly before today, I would not have been able to. But I have learned that in time of war personal happiness comes second and, until the world enemies of peace are forced to capitulate, we will always be at war, cold or hot, in one way or another. But—"

"You haven't liked me," Kitty said abruptly. "No"— she held up a protesting hand as the girl impulsively opened her lips. "Don't try to explain. I understand only too well. I didn't like myself much either. But I had no choice. I came here because I am attached to the government. Since—after Tom—my husband—died I had to find some meaning in my life. Unfortunately, and to our great disappointment, we had no children. More or less by chance I found myself in a position to do a useful piece of work for the British government. After that, they kept me busy. I learned a great deal. The issues at stake were so immense that I learned to see my personal grief in its right perspective, to fill my life with activity that served a real purpose.

"Then I realized that, much as I had loved England, my true home was here in America. I belonged here. My roots were here. So I came back and talked to some government officials in Washington. They knew of my work abroad and decided to use me. When it became known to a certain person in Washington that I had long been acquainted with Donald Garth, he sent me here to help trace the leak through which information was going at the Works. They had men there, of course; then they put Fane in the house, though I did not know myself who he was until just now. They thought I could accomplish things that would be impossible for the men. It was argued that a gay, volatile creature like myself would never be suspected of having any serious purpose.

"Before I came they showed me what information they had collected. There was one name of the many after which they had question marks that was familiar to me. Dick Wentworth. He had several times been seen with one of the men whom

145

they believed to be planted at the Works by the enemy. That was why I added his name to my list of guests for the garden party. Then, too, I was interested in the fact that Dick's former valet had become Don's man. I discovered very soon that Macy was constantly prowling around the house, particularly in the vicinity of the study. The day of the garden party I watched him meet Dick in the most furtive manner—"

"So it was Dick he was with!" Penny exclaimed. "That conversation I heard, 'risky—no other way,' it was—" she broke off. Her mouth was dry and colorless. She forced herself to speak through quivering lips. "I keep trying to realize that it was Dick—Dick and Macy who kidnaped me, struck me, tried to—"

Kitty's small hand that could be so deadly with a revolver touched Penny's shoulder comfortingly. "Yes, it was Dick," she said coolly. "I was almost sure of it. The kidnaping happened on Macy's day off, and when Dick called the next afternoon to see you—good heavens, that was only today, yesterday, I mean," she said, glancing at the clock on Don's desk which showed three o'clock.

"Dick let slip the fact he knew something had happened to you. I suppose he was checking to make sure you had not recognized him. He still hoped, if he could bring you around, to marry you and get Don's money. The way he humiliated Don at the garden party—"

Penny flared. "Nonsense!" she interrupted passionately. "He could not humiliate Don!"

Kitty laughed. "I am glad you realize what a giant of a man you have married." She sobered. "Well, my work here is done." She straightened her slim shoulders wearily. "Don't hate me too much for my interference." A smile of ineffable sweetness lighted her eyes and her lips.

With a swift impulse Penelope kissed her. "Hate you!" she echoed. "Oh, I don't. But what will you do now—Geoff!" she exclaimed. "Geoff was watching Don for the FBI—"

"Geoff!" Kitty was startled. Her eyes opened wide.

"He loves you so much, Kitty," Penny said impulsively.

"I know," Kitty said.

"Can't you make him happy?"

"He thinks I am a fluttery, idle woman. He loves me for that. If he knew what I am really like, he wouldn't want me."

Penny shook her head. "He'd love you so much more if he could see you as I see you now."

Kitty stood, looking unseeingly at the disorder in the study, the jagged pieces of broken glass, the upset chairs, the torn draperies and disorderly papers.

"Tell him how you feel," Penny said suddenly. "Tell him now. Perhaps personal happiness mustn't come first but—it can come second, can't it?"

Kitty's smile was dazzling. "I'll tell him," she said. She gathered up her long skirts and ran, skimming through the study. At the door she blew Penny a kiss. Flung open the door. Gasped.

Geoff was sitting in his wheelchair, the revolver in his hand, and behind him, her hands on the bar that pushed it, white-faced but steadfast, stood Mrs. Owens.

"Geoff!" Kitty cried. "Mother!"

Her mother laughed softly at her expression. "Somewhere in me, Kitty," she said, "there must be an adventurous streak like yours. When I heard you slip downstairs tonight, after we were supposed to be locked in our rooms, I couldn't stay behind. I went in to Geoff and found him almost raving at being out of things. So I pushed his chair into the elevator and we waited here to stop anyone coming out."

Geoff put the revolver away. "There have been times in the last few days," he admitted, "when I suspected you of being an enemy agent." He laughed joyously. "But from what I can make out, you and I should have been partners long ago."

Kitty, recalling the conversation he must have overheard, blushed deeply. Her mother touched her arm. "Kitty," she said, "I've been so worried about you since you came here, the change bothered me. I never guessed—" She brushed her hand across her wet lashes. "I'm so proud of you, dear," she said simply.

Kitty threw her arms around her mother with a little sob. "I couldn't tell you," she said.

"Of course. I understand."

"But you can tell me something, can't you?" Geoff said. Kitty looked at him. Looked away.

With a smile trembling at her lips Mrs. Owens turned and went quietly up the stairs.

"What are you going to tell me?" Geoff said firmly.

"I—I—"

Penny moved toward the door. Closed it. As she did so she heard Geoff say, "Come here to me, Kitty." There was a little pause, a tentative footstep. Then Geoff's voice, muffled, "If you can't tell me, I'll prompt you. I love you, Kitty."

147

XXII

A week later the doctor smiled down at Penny as she lay on the neat hospital bed, and put away his stethoscope.

"Well, young lady," he said cheerfully, "I can't find much wrong with you. Though I must admit you are the worst patient I ever had. If I'd known you would go gallivanting around the woods at night, getting mixed up in a gun battle, and heaven knows what all, I'd have had you brought here in the first place."

Penny laughed at his expression and he scowled at her with pretended sternness. "Saucy, aren't you? Well, you don't deserve your luck, that's all I've got to say." He became serious. "You'll continue to notice that concussion for some time. I want your promise now that you will be sensible."

"I promise," Penny told him.

He looked at her shrewdly. "That's good enough for me. Never knew you to break your word."

"And how soon can I leave? If you knew how well I feel—"

"Today," the doctor said. "Your maid Nora brought your clothes from Uplands for you." His smile broadened. "And what's more—I'm going to have another empty hospital bed today."

"Mother!" Penny said with a squeal of delight.

"As soon as you have dressed you can go in to see her and say good-by before she leaves for the airport, if you like."

"Marmee isn't going alone, is she?" Penny asked anxiously.

The door banged open and Nora appeared, flushed with excitement. She was dressed in a dark-blue suit and wore a smart hat. She carried a suitcase.

"Nora! How smart you look."

Nora beamed. "What do you think, Penny—Mrs. Garth?" The doctor went out with a wave of his hand, closing the door behind him. "Guess what," Nora went on. "Mr. Garth is sending me on the trip with Mrs. Sherrod."

"Oh, Nora, how perfect! You'll give her better care than anyone else possibly could and it will be a wonderful trip for both of you. I'm so happy about it!"

"Well," Nora said briskly, to cover her emotion, "you'd better get dressed if you're going to see your mother. We have a plane to catch. Your mother's all ready and waiting in a wheelchair. I brought your clothes." She did not quite meet Penny's eyes.

Without looking at the girl she unpacked and laid out the clothes. Penny stared in amazement at the filmy underwear, the white tulle dress.

"Heavens, Nora," she protested. "It's lovely—the daintiest thing I ever saw—but I can't wear that to the airport. It looks," she added faintly, "almost like a wedding dress."

Nora, bustling about the hospital room, was silent for a moment. "Mr. Garth said to pick out something suitable," she said at last, without turning around. "Anyhow, you aren't to go to the airport. Your mother will say good-by to you here. She says farewells at trains and planes and boats make her sad and this is to be a joyous occasion."

"But—"

"You go ahead and get dressed," Nora said, flustered. "You mustn't keep your mother waiting."

Penny put on the white tulle dress and looked at herself in the mirror. Was this the same girl who had looked out at her on her wedding day? What was the difference? This girl's eyes sparkled, her lips were warm and curved in a smile. She was glowing. Penny studied her for a long time. Picture of a woman in love, she thought.

Then she curtsied gravely to the shadow woman in white, "Good morning, Mrs. Garth," she said.

Her mother and Nora were waiting in the solarium, her mother sitting in a wheelchair, looking frail, but with glowing eyes. She was anticipating her trip eagerly. Her eyes filled with tears as Penny came in.

"You look like a bride in that dress, dear," she said. "More like a bride, even, than you did in your wedding dress."

"Time to go," the nurse said in a businesslike tone from the doorway.

A firm hand lifted Penny to her feet from her position on her knees beside her mother's chair. Don was standing beside her, very grave, very white, his eyes burning as he looked at her.

When her mother and Nora had taken their leave, Don turned to his wife. "Ready?" he asked. He looked deep into her eyes. "I've come to take you home."

The convertible was waiting and he helped her in. The car moved off smoothly.

"Penny," he began.

"Don," she said breathlessly, "I haven't thanked you for the wonderful flowers you sent while I was in the hospital.

149

There were so many I was able to fill the children's ward."

"Penny," he said again.

"Th-thank you for sending Nora with Marmee. It's a perfect arrangement and will make them both happy. You were very—thoughtful." She looked shyly at him from under her long lashes.

"Penny—" he began for the third time.

Again she forestalled him, almost feverishly. "Don, what about Petro?"

"He's getting better. The doctor removed the bullet. It only grazed his shoulder. He and Geoff have been playing chess and having a fine time while Kitty was getting Geoff's cottage ready for them. They were married this morning."

"I'm glad," Penny said softly. She could feel a blush burning in her cheeks. How long it had taken her to realize why she so disliked Kitty! To know that she had been jealous of her.

"Petro is going to live in that old lodge of mine. We've found out where his family is and arrangements are being made to get them over here."

"I'm terribly glad. We owe him a lot."

"Yes," Don agreed gruffly. "He saved your life. I have a tremendous debt to pay Petro. Perhaps I can help with the education of his brothers and sisters. I've been busy with that and clearing up the legal ends of the Wentworth tangle. That's why I haven't been able to get to the hospital."

"What will happen to him, Don?"

"They are all going to prison," he said curtly.

"What—how did you keep them from getting the blueprints if Macy actually opened your safe?"

Don laughed. "My real safe is built into the back of that monstrosity of a desk chair of mine."

The road widened and there was a parking space looking out upon a view of distant hills. Don swung the car into it, shut off the motor. Turned to her.

"Penny—" This time his tone was so determined that she made no effort to stop him. Her heart was thudding, her breath coming fast through her parted lips. "Penny, there's so much to ask you to forgive me for that I hardly know where to begin."

"Forgive you?" she gasped in amazement.

"Distrusting you, for one thing. You see, I was wildly jealous, and when you went out that night both Kitty and I heard Wentworth's voice somewhere near by."

"Dick Wentworth! But I didn't see him."

150

"I know that now. You were trying, like the magnificently courageous and loyal girl you are, to save both Petro and me. And I—"

"That's over, Don. Let's forget it."

"You mean that?" he said huskily.

"Of course."

"Then, there's something else," he went on more slowly. "That night—was it only a week ago?—when Uplands was raided, Nora found you weren't in your room. I made a terrible choice that night, Penny. I put the country first. I didn't attempt to look for you. I took that chance—"

Penny turned eagerly to face him, her eyes shining, lips tender, so utterly lovely that a lump came into Don's throat.

"Don, that night Petro told me about the choice he had made, putting his country's welfare ahead of his brothers and sisters. He told me—so proudly, Don—that if they knew what he had done they would understand and approve." There was a little pause and then she said softly, "Don, I'm proud, too, and I understand."

He bent over, his face hidden as he held her hand to his lips.

"Penny," he said, "I made a bad mistake once. I fell in love with a girl, fell in love for keeps, but I married her without being sure that she cared for me. That is not a true marriage. I intended to keep you, even when I knew there was someone else in your heart. But it is not fair to you. You have a tremendous gift for loving, Penny. It isn't right to stifle it." He released her hand, gripped the wheel tight. "So if your real happiness lies in your freedom, I will set you free."

Penny's eyes were enormous. She looked at him intently, at the lines of the face she loved. "Is that what you want, Don?" she asked.

"All I want is your happiness."

There was a lovely light in her eyes, her lips curved into an entrancing smile. "Then," she said softly, "then, please— please, don't send me away. Ever."

"Do you mean that?" he asked hoarsely.

"Look at me and see!" she cried joyously.

He turned. Looked at her. Caught her in his arms. "Penny! My darling. My wife!" He kissed her, hair and eyes and chin and lips.

After a moment he released her and then caught her to him again. All the sternness had vanished. He was like a boy, laughing but tender.

"Penny, beloved Penny. We have so much wasted time to make up for."

"But it's all ahead," she said.

"Do you know, the first hope I ever had was the night when Kitty telephoned from Washington and I saw your face. I thought—I hoped—you were a little jealous!"

Penny made a face at him. "I was horribly jealous," she confessed. "But I forgive her now that she's married Geoff."

He lifted her chin, searching her eyes. "Penny." His voice was low, grave. "Do you take this man?"

"Till death us do part," she said softly, "I do."

Something tinkled as he moved and Don bent over to pick it up.

"Why on earth are you carrying that key?"

He turned it over in his hand. "It's the one to the door that connects our rooms. I took it when I locked you in or"—his laughing eyes met hers—"thought I had locked you in that night. I've been carrying it ever since as a sort of talisman." He held it out. "Want it?"

The color deepened in her face. "It belongs to you," she said, and the words were a promise.

Wait 'til you see what *else* we've got in store for you!

Send for your FREE catalog of Bantam Bestsellers today!

This money-saving catalog lists hundreds of best-sellers originally priced from $3.75 to $15.00—yours now in Bantam paperback editions for just 50¢ to $1.95! Here is a great opportunity to read the good books you've missed and add to your private library at huge savings! The catalog is FREE! So don't delay—send for yours today!